DECIMATION

DECIMATION
A NOVEL

R.S. Sodhi

VANTAGE PRESS
New York / Washington / Atlanta
Los Angeles / Chicago

To Santosh and Preeti

FIRST EDITION

All rights reserved, including the right of
reproduction in whole or in part in any form.

Copyright © 1985 by R.S. Sodhi, M.D.

Published by Vantage Press, Inc.
516 West 34th Street, New York, New York 10001

Manufactured in the United States of America
ISBN: 0-533-06429-5

Library of Congress Catalog Card No.: 84-91327

DECIMATION

CHAPTER 1

She was a massive woman. Her thighs were flowing from the sides of the steno chair like the swagged valance of a custom-made drapery. Not without some difficulty, the emergency-room nurse managed to drag herself along with the chair to the Motorola CB radio.

"Metropolitan Hospital. Code Forty-seven," she said.

"Mid-Manhattan ambulance twelve. White male in thirties, unconscious, blood pressure not recordable, pulse feeble. Gunshot wound, abdomen. ETA [estimated time of arrival] five minutes," reported the ambulance attendant.

"Have you got oxygen on?" said the nurse with a Caribbean musical voice. She might have been a chorus girl from a Harry Belafonte show.

"Yes."

"Have you an IV line in?"

"Tried twice. Negative. Veins are collapsed."

The ambulance was screeching down Broadway. Strapped to the stretcher, almost in a coma, Stanley Jacobs could still feel momentary agonizing pains generated by the wheels of the ambulance dipping into potholes on the Manhattan street. He could barely perceive the siren of the ambulance. He opened his eyes and looked out through the darkened windows of the ambulance. The rest of the world was moving in the opposite direction at a maddening pace. One attendant was sitting on a stool near his head. He was trying to adjust two plastic prongs into Jacob's nose to deliver the oxygen. Another one was sitting on a bench by the side of Stanley Jacobs. He was holding Jacobs's hand. He momentarily squeezed the hand.

"Everything is going to be fine," he said. "We will be in the hospital in no time."

With tremendous effort, he opened his eyes. His vision was blurry, still his mind was sharp. He perceived an impotent apprehension flooding the ambulance. His concern had multiplied, for there was nothing else this man could offer him. Somehow he had to cling to life until he reached the hospital. Then everything went blank. He felt an immense pressure on his chest, but there was no pain. From somewhere faraway, he heard a distant voice, "He has arrested, let's start CPR [cardiopulmonary resuscitation]."

The automatic doors of the emergency room flung open. Three attendants wheeled the victim in. The urgency and the concern written over their faces contrasted with the cool and casualness of the doctors and nurses who took over as the patient was transferred onto the emergency-room stretcher. Like participants in a well-rehearsed military mission, they seemed to know their roles precisely.

One nurse had taken hold of an awkward-looking scissor and split the sides of the shirt and the undershirt, not caring about or appreciating the expensive taste of the man wearing them. As she lifted the cut half of the blood-drenched undershirt, right above the umbilicus, there was a wound from which blood was flowing as slowly as if it were going to stop any second.

Dr. Johnson had put a tourniquet on the arm and was waiting impatiently for the vein to blow up, but the vein was taking its own time. The patient was virtually drained of blood.

Another nurse had taken his blood pressure. "Dr. Johnson, I can't get any blood pressure."

Dr. Johnson paid no attention to her. He could tell the patient was in serious trouble, the way his veins were collapsed. He kept concentrating on the needle he was going to insert into the vein. He knew he had to insert the needle as a top priority, for that was going to be the link between the patient and the medications he was going to deliver. As soon as the blood started trickling through the needle, the nurse connected it to a plastic tube descending from a dangling bottle hanging from an unstable hook somewhere above the patient's head.

Hardly a minute had passed. Several residents, interns, and medical students had descended from nowhere.

With the fluid pouring relentlessly through the needle, Dr. Johnson was ready to assume complete control of the command post.

"Doctor," Johnson ordered the intern standing opposite him, "start another IV on the other arm. Make sure you put in a big needle. At least eighteen."

"Type and cross match—several units." This order was not directed at any particular physician.

"His respirations are thirty per minute. Shallow," said the intern standing near the head of the patient.

"Increase the oxygen to ten litres." Dr. Johnson started examining the abdomen, trying to find any areas of tenderness or resistance. "Looks like.24 gun, Saturday-night Special," he muttered to himself. He put a sterile dressing over the wound, secured it with tape, and pointed to the doctor standing by his side. "Put a Foley catheter in."

"What size?"

"I don't care what size. Put any damn tube and leave it in." Dr. Johnson had more things on his mind than telling the intern the size of the catheter.

Dr. Johnson was obviously directing a perfectly organized chaos. There were several doctors and nurses surrounding the patient, inserting needles, taking blood pressure, and adjusting the various contraptions surrounding the patient. Suggestions were pouring in from all directions. "Give him sodium bicarb, decrease the oxygen, put in central venous line, give him plasma, take him to the operating room." Dr. Johnson knew it was prudent to listen to all the suggestions, but it was more important to sift them and reject the ones he thought were unnecessary. As the chief resident of the emergency room, he had the responsibility and final say in the treatment of this patient. Strangely enough, the worst hour in victim Jacobs's life was the finest hour in Dr. Johnson's life, for this was his first attempt at resuscitation since he had become chief resident.

Not out of defiance, but more out of curiosity and indifference, a couple of medical students had moved in front of Dr. Johnson, who with a height of 5 feet 7 inches was cut off from his patient. But that was no problem. Johnson thrust his hands between the two men, shoved them aside, and gained access back to the patient, blurting out, "Only the surgical team stays here. The rest can leave the emergency room."

Dr. Johnson might as well have said nothing, for nobody budged an inch.

"Has anyone taken his arterial blood gases?" asked Dr. Johnson.

"Yes, doctor," replied the nurse who was keeping track of the medication administered and the timing of various procedures.

"Well?" he looked at the nurse.

"I don't have the results yet," said the nurse.

"For God's sake, how long does it take to get the results?" Dr. Johnson knew he had to put some teeth into his waning authority. After all, at this point in time, he was the unquestionable authority in the treatment of this patient.

He examined the patient's head. He felt it all around and mumbled to himself, "Pupils reacting and equal."

There was a ring on the telephone stuck to the wall. The nurse picked up the phone and jotted some numbers. "Doctor, I have the arterial blood gases."

Dr. Johnson looked at the nurse, with the light still directed at the patient's eyes, and waited for the magic numbers.

"PO_2—45," she said.

Dr. Johnson placed the stethoscope on either side of the chest. His face turned ashen gray. "Damn it. No breath sounds on the right side." He shoved the stethoscope into his pocket and elbowed his way to the patient's head. "Nurse, get me an endotracheal tube."

Dr. Johnson bent down and inserted a steel plate, with the lighted end into Jacobs's throat. "I can't get the tube in," he said. "Press down on the trachea." Moments later he stood up straight. "It looks to be in. Can you hear the breath sounds?"

Another doctor put his stethoscope on either side of the chest. "Yes, good air entry both sides."

"All right, inflate the balloon." Dr. Johnson was relieved, for at least he had accomplished this procedure without any delay, for he knew that inserting an endotracheal tube into patient's throat can be a very frustrating experience.

Dr. Johnson looked around. "Who is the chest man here?"

"Over here," gestured the pulmonary surgical resident, a stocky short man whose square glasses seemed so much out of place on his round face.

"No breath sounds on the right side. Absolutely none. I think he needs a chest tube," said Dr. Johnson.

The chest resident pulled out the unlit pipe from his mouth and thrust it into his back pocket. He put his stethoscope on the chest for barely a second or two and walked over to the X-ray view box. "Yup, that lung is completely collapsed. He certainly needs one."

He put on a pair of surgical gloves and abruptly painted the chest with a brown antiseptic in preparation for the insertion of chest tube. He kept on talking, "The bullet must have penetrated the diaphragm and injured the right lung." If these comments were meant for Dr. Johnson, he didn't hear them, for he was giving undivided attention to Dr. Chimanski, the surgeon, who had just walked in.

Stanley Jacobs lay there, his face turning paler every minute. Life was quickly vanishing out of him. His blood pressure had stayed down. A machine had taken over his breathing. Consciousness level had not improved. Dr. Johnson stood there helpless, not knowing the next move to resuscitate his patient.

Saturated with clinical data supplied by Dr. Johnson, Dr. Chimanski walked toward the patient. Imperceptibly, a chasm had appeared in the human mass surrounding the patient, providing him an easy access to the patient. He examined the abdomen of the patient. Silence had suddenly descended. He put his stethoscope on the chest. He kept on listening for a few seconds, and then almost instantaneously, while keeping the chest piece firmly on the chest, raised his eyebrows and rolled up his eyes as far as they would go, looking at the doctor standing in front of him. That immediately killed the whispering noise coming from the crowd.

Dr. Chimanski looked at Johnson. "How much urine has he put out?"

"None so far," said Dr. Johnson.

"Who shot him?"

Before anyone could reply, Dr. Chimanski had walked to the x-ray view box. "So the man is shot. Within minutes his blood pressure drops into his shoes. You haven't been able to resuscitate him in all the time you had. X ray shows the bullet in the midline. We don't have the side view, of course. Johnson, what about his femoral arteries?"

"I haven't felt them yet." His voice hardly audible.

Chimanski looked at Johnson as though he was the most careless creature on this planet. "I don't believe it, Dr. Johnson. You should know by now that this is one of the most important parts of the examination in an abdominal trauma."

Chimanski briskly pressed his fingers in each groin. He pulled Johnson to the side. "You do not need to be a doctor but a plumber to know a simple fact. If there is no water in the faucet, there is a leak in the pipe. This man has no femorals. There is a leak on the way. Obviously the same plumber would tell you that the leak needs to be plugged. You can pump all the blood you have in New York into this man, he will not recover. Obviously he has injured a major blood vessel. Promise me one thing, Doctor. In the future, you will use your brain. Right now, let's take him to the operating room immediately."

"His blood pressure is not recordable," said the nurse.

Dr. Chimanski ignored that information. "Okay, let's wheel him to the operating room."

Insisted the nurse, "Doctor, I don't have the permission from the relatives." Dr. Chimanski looked at the nurse, his eyes bulging out as if they had been instantaneously pushed out by a forceful pump sitting behind them. The cool and confident look of the strange mixture of black and brown of his eyes was suddenly transformed by that force into anger and frustration.

"Nurse, I don't need any silly permission to operate on this man. Get me the operating room and get me an anesthesiologist. That is all I ask of you." He turned toward Dr. Johnson. "He should not have been kept here for such a long time. By now he should have been opened up."

As the disorganized procession moved along the corridor, Dr. Chimanski merely moved along, confident that the chaotic transfer was not going to harm his patient. The intern who was pulling on the oxygen tank connected to the patient had gone out of pace with the mass movement, with the result that he almost yanked the endotracheal tube out of Jacobs's throat. It continued through the narrow corridors, which, it seemed, weren't designed for the mechanical and human medical paraphernalia accompanying the patient.

As they reached the end of the corridor, one of the doctors looked down the criss-cross bars of the elevator door. There was loud conversation in Spanish ascending from the basement along the shaft of the elevator. He started pounding on the bars of the door of the elevator for it to be sent up immediately. The conversation in Spanish abruptly stopped. The elevator operator shouted back in broken English that the elevator was out of order and insisted that the doctor stop pounding on the door. Then the procession moved directly to the next elevator leading to the operating room. When they reached the operating room, most of the doctors and nurses turned back and Dr. Chimanski disappeared into the changing room. Dr. Johnson replayed the whole incident in his own mind, trying to find any hidden compliments from Dr. Chimanski, for he thought he had done a pretty good job of treating this patient.

The nurse pushed the switch. A large circular disk, suspended from the ceiling by a sturdy green rod, lit up. She adjusted the light and focused a circular beam over the bullet wound. The assisting surgeon had positioned himself opposite Dr. Chimanski, on the other side of the operating table. He sterilized the abdomen with an antiseptic and neatly arranged the sterile towels, leaving a bare rectangular area around the wound. He was intense and nervous. Scattered beads of perspiration had already appeared on his brow, partly soaked up by the surgical cap.

Dr. Chimanski thrust his hands into the surgical gloves. His brain was racing through the possible internal injuries and quickly scanning the various choices he had. Torn aorta. No question he had to put in the arterial graft.

Injured intestines. Exteriorize the bowel as colostomy or completely close the abdomen?

Antibiotics. During or after the surgery or wait and see?

Would he go into a shock lung? Should he give steroids?

Kidneys. Would they shut down? If they did, he knew his problems were going to be unbelievable.

He had examined all the options and made up his mind. He took a few steps toward the patient. He surveyed the wound and looked at the anesthesiologist.

"Tell me when," said Chimanski.

The anesthesiologist nodded, "Go ahead."

Chimanski made a long incision and opened the magic box.

It was difficult to imagine an invalid, much less dying, Stanley Jacobs lying on the operating table. He was connected to machines that had arbitrarily split his body into different components. The respiratory system, the cardiovascular system, and so forth. This was pitiable, for the whole Jacobs was a dynamic man who had kept pace with the most powerful people, be they in the White House, Senate, or various governments on the other side of the world. He was a man in perpetual motion, being whisked from one five-star hotel to the other, at a speed greater than that of sound. A multimillion deal clinched in London at breakfast. Same day at lunch, in Zurich, thumbs down on a deal of similar dimensions.

Perhaps his greatest asset was that his position wasn't inherited or bought with the influence of wealth, but rather through the persistence of hard work. Seven years earlier he had moved to New York from the West Coast. Then, he was penniless. His first job in New York was running a hot-dog stand on Forty-second Street in front of movie houses and other houses of questionable repute. Two years later, he had acquired several fast-food restaurants. Then he joined the Sea Cola Corporation. Now, at the age of forty, he was the vice-president of the Sea Cola Corporation. Five feet ten inches tall, always immaculately dressed, he had dark brown hair and dark eyes set in perfectly shaped sockets, with strong cheekbones, the sort of appearance that didn't arouse compassion in the people around, but demanded order and discipline.

It had been in his first year as the vice-president when Owen Williams, the president of the company, had called him.

Owen had exploded, "Credibility or no credibility, the interests of the company must be protected."

He looked at Williams with his piercing dark eyes as if he was zeroing somewhere deep inside him. The rest of his face stayed calm, like an Indian etched on the totem pole.

"I have promised the Sea Cola plant to the Spanish government. Can't go back on my word," said Jacobs.

"Damn your word, Stan. Not going to risk ten million dollars in Spain."

"Let me put it this way, Owen," he told Williams tersely. "I give you twenty-four hours. If you do not back me, I will resign tomorrow morning."

The left side of his mouth separated a little and pulled to the left side. Owen wasn't sure whether he was ridiculing or if it was a mannerism of no significance at all.

"Stanley Jacobs, get this straight." He stood up from his chair. His face was red. His brain was simmering with anger. Business matters, he could take care of. He was capable of twisting arms and sweetening deals, And occasionally, in the name of sound business judgment, crawling on the carpet. Here the situation was different. Jacobs was insisting on a business deal based on ethics rather than dollars and cents.

"Get this straight," he continued. "my ancestors have invested theirs and I have invested my life in this company. We have built this empire through sound judgment, not through credibility jargon."

Jacobs was losing patience. He thrust his hand at Williams.

His facial expressions became symmetrical. A perfectly organised smile appeared on his face. Suddenly he knew he was right. He was supremely confident. He glanced right through Williams and focused on a distant world.

He said calmly, "My credibility is not for auction."

"Neither is my company," replied Williams.

"Take it or leave it. Your choice." Jacobs walked out of the room.

Before the clock struck nine, Williams had called Jacobs. He had never regretted that, for two years' investment had racked in a profit of four million.

His immense wealth, power, and charm were all there to convert people into diminutive puppets so that when the time came to hit a target, or, for that matter, to protect a target, all he had to do was to pull the right string. He was aloof. His judgment wasn't slanted by an intriguing wife or conspiring girlfriend, for he had neither. For hours at a time, he would walk in the snow near his country home, extracting answers from the wilderness. People had nothing to offer him. Like Williams, they were tiny soldiers in his vast power game. But solitude was there to replenish his depleted energy. Then he would be back in New York. For unsurmountable problems, which his assistants had so classified, instantaneous answers would emerge. Magic was in all those little strings.

When not on business assignments, he would get into his private airplane and fly to the central part of New York State to his favorite estate overlooking the Mohawk Valley. Most of the time, he would be sitting in front of the fireplace, sipping martinis, writing figures on paper, which were hard to understand, and then destroying them in the fire, his left hand gently caressing his eyebrows, his eyes fixed on the paper in an expressionless stance. Then, after a while, a gleam would appear in his eyes. A sense of self-assurance was then obvious, around him, and finally he would get up with his drink, looking out of the window with that rare combination of caution, confidence, and fear, as if he were trying to size up a hostile world. Business circles knew that his famous Sea Cola strategies originated from this weekend resort.

If business circles had any doubts about his ability, they had been dispelled the previous month when Jacobs was invited to the White House at the State Dinner given in honor of Mr. Mullinkolv, the Chairman of the Soviet Union. When Jacobs was introduced to him, a crude and broad smile had appeared on Mr. Mullinkolv's chubby face and he chuckled, "Tell me, Mr. Jacobs, how did you fulfill your American dream?"

Jacobs wasn't sure whether to take this as a compliment or a taunt. In a lesser situation, he probably would have pulled out some punches. "In five years, from nowhere I have become one of the richest and most successful persons in the United States." Jacobs smiled a little. He knew this answer was going to please Mullinkolv, for the Communists like to see themselves above and immune to the infection of wealth. But still he wasn't sure whether this would lock the horns.

Mullinkolv was not going to give up. "Mr. Jacobs, obviously we differ on what constitutes success and dreams, but I do admire you."

Jacobs had no intention of demonstrating one-upmanship with Chairman Mullinkolv. He was glad the conversation had moved back to mutual complimentary status. He said, "Mr. Mullinkolv, sir, we appreciate your tireless efforts to bring this world to an era of lasting peace."

Mullinkolv handed him a bottle of Russian vodka. The Stolichnaya Vodka Company was celebrating its three-hundredth anniversary.

That only meant one thing on the stock exchange. The Sea Cola shares had rocketed beyond the reach of a common investor. The Russians were ready to open the doors to the Sea Cola Corporation. This was a big breakthrough for Jacobs, for it was only a matter of time before he could negotiate a Sea Cola plant in Russia.

By 4:00 A.M. the effect of the anesthetic was wearing off. Jacobs tried to open his eyes. They felt heavy and relaxed. He felt his own shallow warm breath deflected against his nose. In fact he felt so relaxed, it was as if every muscle fiber in his body had been specially treated and put into a state of extreme relaxation. His mind was drifting in a sea of tranquility. Nothing, absolutely nothing, disturbed that drift. After a while the subconscious part of his psyche started awakening. The instinctive desires and drives, which are so primitive in a man, appeared on the surface. His ego, which had suppressed these desires for a long time, was still in deep slumber under the effect of the anesthetic. He was moving about in bed, not so much in distress, but more in primitive anger. He was mumbling incoherently, which the nurse in his room did not understand. She was so used to incoherent utterances of patients coming out of anesthesia that it made no sense to her. Her concern was mainly centered in checking his vital signs and making sure the machinery around the patient functioned properly.

As the anesthetic wore off further, the relaxation was replaced by an ache all over the body. He took a deep breath and felt an abrupt sharp pain in his abdomen and opened his eyes. Everything around him was hazy and out of focus as though someone had taken a snapshot through a cheap camera. That earlier feeling of tranquility had left him, and he lay there in the small cubicle of the intensive-care unit surrounded by off-white curtains. He wanted to drift back into that tranquility, but the sickening feeling in his abdomen was too distracting. He looked around at the various tubes and medical contraptions invading his body. He knew something had drastically gone wrong. On either side there were innumerable plastic tubes descending from somewhere and disappearing under his bedsheets. There was large empty space in front of him. Further up there was a glass partition behind which doctors and nurses were jumbled together looking at the monitors, as if a space ship was about to take off. He tried to lift his hands, but he couldn't. They were strapped and tied to the bed railings.

"Mr. Jacobs, you are in the intensive-care unit. You had surgery for a gunshot wound of the abdomen. Your abdomen will be sore for a while," the nurse tried to reassure Jacobs.

Jacobs closed his eyes. He wanted to drift back into that wonderland.

"Mr. Jacobs, if your abdomen is hurting you, please let me know. I will give you an injection."

Jacobs opened his eyes and took a deep breath. He felt

sickening pain in his abdomen. "What happened, Nurse?"

"Someone shot you. Dr. Chimanski did the surgery. Everything is all right now. Who is your nearest relative? Whom do you want us to notify?"

Jacobs said nothing. He simply stared ahead.

The nurse was disappointed. She had planned answers to all the possible questions that her patient might have. She had planned to minimize the gravity of the situation. She had planned to dodge questions of any significance, which she thought should be best left to Dr. Chimanski. But Jacobs had no questions.

He started recollecting what exactly happened. He last remembered sitting in the theatre watching a ballet. He had walked out of the theatre onto Forty-second Street. It was an unusually warm December day. There was a slight drizzle, which wasn't enough to drive people off the streets, but still it was annoying. There was that mild fog in the street. The moon, far away, looked impotent trying to penetrate that fog. He walked into the telephone booth and made a telephone call. He heard a tap on the door of the phone booth. He could not see the outside clearly. His vision was partly obscured by the smoke he had generated from the pipe he was smoking and partly from his breath, which had laid a thin layer of moisture inside the glass. He thought he had taken too much time making the call. This was Christmas Eve. Maybe there was a man or someone impatient to hurry home to celebrate the birth of Christ or maybe there was someone who had a little too much to drink and was getting edgy in the drizzle outside. There was another tap on the door. He rubbed the inside of the glass and through a small window thus created he looked out. There was a black boy in his teens outside, his nose pressed into a small circle against the door. Those dark eyes were staring at him. He remembered them so well, for they were the only things he could see outside the booth. There were bright red blood vessels on the white of his eyes, which appeared like tortuous streams going in all directions and finally disappearing under his lids. He opened the door. He felt something sticking in his abdomen. He looked down. There was a gun pointed at him.

"Mister, hand me your wallet and you won't be hurt." The

boy was nervous. Jacobs felt the tremor of the barrel against his flesh.

The boy was standing so close to him that he could smell the obnoxious smell of sweat on him. For a moment he thought it could be a toy gun and felt like punching the boy, but there was no point in taking a chance. That could be a dangerous move. People on the street were completely unaware of the hold-up. He hoped someone would soon spot the gun. Jacobs inserted his hand into the inside pocket. The boy pushed the gun further into his flesh. He cautioned, "Don't do anything stupid." He thrust his hand in Jacobs's pocket and pulled the wallet out. "Now close the door and stay in. You won't be hurt."

Jacobs felt the pressure of the gun disappearing. He closed the door. The boy ran toward the car parked nearby. Suddenly Jacobs remembered he had important papers in the wallet. He came out of the telephone booth. He stopped, for he had seen a hand appearing through the side window of the back seat of the car. Then he heard a loud thunder. For a few seconds, he stood there, stunned by the excruciating pain. His legs were carrying a ton of weight. His knees buckled under, and he fell on the pavement. He lay on the pavement thinly covered with mushy snow, close to the road. He put his hand on the abdomen. Warm blood was gushing out of the abdomen, rushing along the pavement to the gutter alongside the road, there mixing with slush of snow and salt. As the cars passed by, they threw a spray of slush onto him and the people who had surrounded him. Jacobs didn't care. Everything around him was hazy. Everyone was moving in a slow motion.

The show in the movie had just finished. As he turned his head to the side, he saw a sudden surge of a million legs moving toward him. But in a short while they had all disappeared along with the distracting noise. The intense pain had vanished. He didn't feel the cold pavement anymore. As he looked through the crowded heads of the people around him, he saw the tall buildings swinging to and fro in a rhythmic manner as if they had life of their own. There was perpetual noise around him, but he didn't care. There were black spots floating everywhere around him. He was almost in a coma.

The nurse interrupted his train of thoughts. "Mr. Jacobs, I am going to give you an injection to relieve the pain."

Jacobs felt helpless lying in the intensive-care unit, surrounded by machines that appeared so alien. For the first time in his life, he was not controlling the events around him and his own existence seemed insignificant. He had become silly putty in the hands of fate, being twisted into shapes and sizes by an unknown force over which he had no control. One moment, perhaps, he was the most precious man, the next moment had transformed him into insignificant creature, by a cruel stroke of luck. He thought that could be the cause of inertia of most of the people on this earth. Their existence was unpredictable. Only if he had not gone after the boy, how different things would be. At that moment he had lost logic, and this was the price he was paying for it. Still, thank God, he was alive and could pick up the pieces.

The narcotic injection was taking effect. He was drifting into a world of confused thoughts so indescribable yet so beautiful. Everyone else in his room seemed out of tune with his new-found world under the narcotics. What right had they to destroy serenity so heavenly! He was slowly drifting into a world of oblivion.

CHAPTER 2

Early in the morning, there was a strange quietness interrupted periodically by sounds generated by the machines. The mechanical little monsters, with a language of their own, had taken over the intensive-care unit completely. Every human soul around had willingly accepted a secondary role, faithfully responding to the hissing, beeping, clicking sounds and bizarre yellow writings on the green dials. Only when the human response was lagging or insufficient, the monsters would yell out a loud command, triggering off a stampede response from the doctors and the nurses.

It was the twenty-fifth of December. Not that the intensive-care unit exhibited any indication of the birth of Christ except for a wreath stuck to the door of the ICU. On either side there were off-white curtains separating Jacobs from other patients. From behind one of them, there was rhythmic hissing sound from a respirator, sounding as if a cobra had been trapped in that cubicle. Straight ahead, in the wide space, doctors, nurses, and technicians were all moving in different directions. They had all conspired against a coordinated effort.

The effect of the anesthetic had completely disappeared. Reality had finally raised its ugly head. One damn mistake and he was paying such a heavy price. For that fraction of a second, instinct had overpowered his logic and that meant a bullet in his abdomen. Looking back, after all, there was nothing in his wallet worth risking his life for. Those insignificant punks had messed up his life.

"I am Dr. Chimanski. We met last night, but I don't expect

you to remember that." Jacobs turned his head to one side. How the six-foot-tall doctor had crept through his field of vision, he could not understand. Jacobs tried to smile, but his crusty dry lips just would not part.

"How do you feel this morning?" asked Chimanski, a subtle blend of dark and brown in his eyes displaying a compassion and genuine concern for his patient. He had a matching color of his hair, except for the temples where premature gray streaks had appeared.

"My stomach is so sore, you dare not touch it with a feather," said Jacobs.

Chimanski had assured Jacobs that, barring any unforeseen circumstances, his recovery would be all right. He had gone into considerable length detailing the extent of the injuries jumping from medical language to layman's explanation, leaving Jacobs confused except for the fact he realized that the biggest artery in his body was torn apart and Chimanski had to put in a graft to repair the damage. Under usual circumstances Chimanski would not have gone to that extent, but this was a special patient. The media had taken an extraordinary interest in the shooting, which wasn't surprising, for Jacobs was a business tycoon and had the connections in the right places in both the Senate and the White House.

"Doctor, when do I get rid of these tubes?"

"Not a minute later than necessary," Chimanski attempted to dodge the question.

A momentary burst of energy had overtaken Jacobs. Although hoarse, his voice was commanding now. "Wait a minute, Doctor. Can you be more specific?"

"Well, the tube coming out of your nose will be out tomorrow. The one draining your urine, hopefully, the day after. The rest we have to play by ear."

"What about this tube coming out of the chest? Every time I take a deep breath, it feels someone is plunging a six-inch knife in there. Did the bullet damage my lungs?"

Chimanski sat on the chair near the bed. "No. Luckily, the bullet never left your abdomen. You have what we call tension pneumothorax. You have a couple of broken ribs, and these broken ribs punctured your lung. I presume that happened from the impact of the fall against the pavement."

Deep inside Chimanski knew it wasn't the impact that caused the fracture but the overenthusiastic resuscitation by the ambulance attendants who had leaned so hard on his chest, they had broken the ribs and punctured the lung.

Continued Chimanski, "But this is a minor setback. I will pull the tube out in a couple of days."

"Dr. Chimanski, I understand the press has been hounding the hospital."

"Yes, they have been. And talking of that, why, I got a call from . . . " Chimanski pulled a partly crushed paper from his pocket. "Call from Mr. Williams. Is that the right name? Would you believe at 4:00 A.M.? He wanted to know how you were and to convey best wishes for your recovery. He is the president of Sea Cola, isn't he?"

"You are partly right. But actually, he owns the company," said Jacobs.

"Anyway, he said he would cut short his visit in Switzerland and would be back in New York tomorrow."

"Do you know whether the police got the muggers?" asked Jacobs.

"I have no idea, but there is a policeman in the lobby. He wants to talk to you. Mr. Jacobs, who do you want us to notify regarding your injuries?"

"No one." Jacobs simply looked ahead.

"Are you married?" Chimanski wasn't sure whether he was asking the right question.

"No."

"Do you have any relatives we can contact?" insisted Chimanski.

"No." He looked at Chimanski, his eyes narrowed to bring him into proper focus. He knew the time had come to stop Chimanski's questioning. "And you do not have to pity me. The isolation is self-imposed."

This was a good lesson for Chimanski. Getting involved

with patients' problems was one thing, but invasion of their privacy quite another.

"I am sorry. I understand." Chimanski had realized this wasn't his usual garden-variety patient. This was at least a multimillionaire, and they had their own reasons for idiosyncrasies and, who knows, perhaps their own reasons to get shot.

"Dr. Chimanski. You can brief the press as you see fit," said Jacobs.

"Any restrictions?" This time Chimanski was not going to take any chances with Jacobs. He wanted to be sure.

"I will leave that to your discretion."

Jacobs lay there like an expensive IBM computer, temporarily defunct from a short circuit, but ready to spring into action as soon as repairs were completed. But Chimanski knew, in spite of his patient's tremendous emotional stability, even he had a breaking point. However, with this mental attitude, he was going to make a fast recovery. Chimanski walked out of the ICU partly numb, partly amazed, following his brief encounter with this tycoon. He took the elevator to the basement and went into the coffee shop. As he sipped coffee, his brief encounter with Jacobs still clouded his mind. Here was a man shot night before, still not out of danger, yet he exhibited no emotion, only perfect logic, leading to precise questioning. He shook his head side to side, contemplating what industrial society had done to this man. Strange price for progress, as if the society had engaged a surgeon to precisely and neatly excise emotions, leaving behind a man cool with logic and determination. That was probably the price of success of business executives.

That evening, when Chimanski had finished watching his interview on the television regarding Stanley Jacobs, the full impact of the events of the previous twenty-four hours permeated his consciousness. It was only a stroke of luck that he had been chosen to operate on Jacobs. If Jacobs had a choice, he would not have come to this city hospital and certainly would have asked for a more experienced surgeon.

As he lay on the sofa, listening to the Russian music, his thoughts turned to his early life in Soviet Union. His parents, in the city of Kiev, were complete strangers to him. His mother, a petite and fragile woman, had spent her life in a struggle just to exist. As a far back in his childhood as he could remember, his mother was hovering around somewhere in the periphery whereas the State was in the center of the arena directing his various moves. Father was different. He was tall and fat and disproportionately developed. Where his mother was unsure of her moves and fumbled in the society, his father thrived under the same circumstances. He had found the right ingredients for success. His first ingredient was the unquestionable allegiance to the government. Second was vodka, which numbed his rebellious urges and sharpened his commitment to authority. All this, no small feat. With his meager education, he had become Deputy Commissar of Kiev. Next step to chief Commissar was only a matter of time. He had believed that the way to reform and change a person is not through intellectual discussions but through the stick.

It had been a bitterly cold February evening. Olig was eleven years old then. From school he had trudged through deep snow and walked into the house. His father had caught hold of back of his collar and dragged him into the family room.

"What did you ask your teacher?" he inquired.

"Papa, I—"

Olig was trembling. His tongue was paralyzed. A fierce hurricane was shaking him. He knew he could not stop it. From his past experience, he knew that the elements of the brutal force were all there. Father's red fiery eyes, the half-finished bottle of vodka, and finally that incident in school.

Then he felt something on his temple. It wasn't so much the pain, but the explosion within his head. Was there another blow? He wasn't sure. He was lying on the floor. He looked up. The huge monster had his eyes fixed on him. They reflected a desire partially fulfilled, the rest still to be fulfilled.

He clung to his huge legs, "Pardon me, Papa."

Instantaneously, his father lifted his leg and next moment

Olig was flying through the air and hitting the opposite wall. For the time being, it was all over. Olig didn't feel the pain. The torment of agony and anticipation were gone. He was unconscious.

The mother had finally picked up enough courage. She came and put his bleeding head in her lap.

"You didn't have to hit him," she said.

"This pygmy"—he gulped down the rest of vodka, some of it drooling from the sides of his mouth, and wiped it off with one quick swipe of the cuff of his shirt—"is going to cost me my job."

"We can talk to him," she pleaded.

His fiery red eyes transformed into glowing fire.

"You spoiled him. How can I talk sense with this kid? He asked his teacher why we can't have free elections."

"He is only a child."

"Some child." He wagged the bottle at her. "In this country six-year-old kids know better. They don't goad and provoke authority."

He dragged both of them out of the room and threw the bottle smashing after them. He closed the door and reached for another bottle.

Father was right. He was the law-enforcement officer of the city. His job was to make sure no one stepped out of line. Here, his own son, was probing dangerous horizons.

Next morning a neighbor had found him lying face down in a heap of snow. His body was cold and rigid.

"Has been dead for several hours," the doctor had declared.

Against his own free will, Olig had been set free, as if an exorcist had banished the evil spirit. He had buried himself in his books and at the age of seventeen was admitted to medical school in Moscow.

Next year, at the age of eighteen, he had gone home for the holidays. He distinctly remembered the day he had met his wife, Zenia. It was an October evening. The fiftieth anniversary of the Bolshevik Revolution was being celebrated in the community hall. At one time, before the Revolution, this had been a church.

From the outside, everything was same as before, except that the cross on the front had been ripped off and the sickle and hammer was nailed in its place. Inside, the stained-glass windows, as the time progressed, had been broken and replaced by plain glass. The thick wooden floor had a million dents from the steel-toed shoes of the soldiers. They used this place for a variety of reasons.

But tonight this place had a different style. The fiftieth anniversary of the revolution was being celebrated. Suddenly tonight the community had lost its subdued character. The spirit of celebration had overtaken everyone, considerably helped by the free vodka provided by the State. In one corner, either by design or just negligence, there were two steel rings hanging from two sturdy ropes going over large pulleys. Chimanski, at that time, had no idea what this was all about, but three years later in Siberia when they tied his hands to similar-looking rings and pulled the rope leaving him, suspended in the air, he knew what it was all about.

The evening had started with the fine Russian music, but by ten o'clock, the effect of the combination of enthusiasm and unlimited quantities of vodka had peaked. Their clatter, their shouts, and their boisterousness had completely overshadowed the music. People on the dance floor, if they had any rhythm, had lost it now. The Russian tradition of fine music, accompanied by graceful dancing with a touch of flair, was as if butchered with indifference in this hall tonight. The boisterous crowd had acquired an uninhibited character, like a carnival celebration following a cattle auction. The crowd had no style and no rhythm, only life.

He remembered standing in a corner and drawing on a cigarette. Across the hall he had seen a face, serene, calm, and innocent, her dark eyes dissipating a strange phenomenon permeating the hall, as if in their own way throwing a challenge to this unruly crowd, being the only particle of sanity surviving in this hall. Her impact was so strong, he had obliterated the crowd out of his mind. He walked over to her. As he introduced himself, he noticed he had overrated her calmness. There was tremor on her lips and quiver in her voice. As they danced, with the exception of the music, the rest of the world had vanished.

This place wasn't meant for either one of them. They walked out of the hall. The crisp October air had not yet developed a biting character. Hand in hand they walked down the pavement. The noise from the hall had faded, replaced by the thrilling calmness of the moonlight reflected off the golden autumn leaves spread all around.

She wasn't beautiful, but attractive and understanding, the sort of person who would adapt to any surprises in life that may have in store. When he completed his medical studies in Moscow, they were married. He started practice in Kiev. That was the most satisfying time of his life. He was at peace with himself. His wife was understanding. Above all, he loved medicine. His passion for medicine, his love for his wife, and his concern for his patients had all merged to form his sphere, which did not need any tricks or intrigues to stabilize its existence. But then there were forces outside this sphere that had different designs for Chimanski. They were there to remind him that he belonged to the State, that he had a greater responsibility to the State than to his patients.

He had hardly finished the first year of his practice when a man was brought to him to be certified mentally incompetent so that he could be placed in an institution. Chimanski examined him and found no trace of mental illness. The man was a physicist. His views were certainly at variance with the authorities. When Chimanski refused to certify him insane, threats started coming in from the local government. When he refused to change his mind, a week later, two KGB agents picked him up at the hospital and took him to Moscow.

In Moscow he was tried for reactionary activities. For three days he sat in the court listening to ridiculous accusations. He was sure the judge would realize the absurdity of the accusations, but he was wrong. He was found guilty of reactionary activities and sentenced to hard labor in Siberia for five years. When he asked the judge what reactionary activities he was found guilty of, he just smiled, got up from his chair and walked away.

What about his wife? What about his patients? Everything had to wait until he was fit to get back into the Russian mainstream.

The day he landed in Siberia the systematic process had started to break his soul and break his soul they did. Tonight, while lying on the sofa, he remembered the prison warden in Siberia. He was a merciless man who would abuse, kick around, and conduct summary executions of the hard-core political prisoners. His philosophy and mission were identical. He was there to convert intellectuals, through whatever means, to regimented communistic philosophy and those who did not bend were liquidated. At first Chimanski resisted. But soon his conscience started buckling under the pressure of starvation and physical abuse.

One year had passed. He had realized that his philosophy of simple and ethical medical practice had landed him in enough trouble with the State. He had finally come around to the fact individual had no right or respect, for the State had monopoly on both. Now, in his life, to stay alive had become a top priority. He knew the time had come to mortgage his soul to stay physically intact. As soon as he accepted the State's supreme authority over the individual, the prison warden's attitude toward him changed. The warden had broken down another reactionary and reformed him into a faithful Communist. He was no longer physically abused. He was getting more to eat. His frostbitten toes had respite, for he was allowed to work indoors. But he still admired those prisoners who had refused to barter their consciences for a few extra slices of bread.

Two years later he was transferred back to Kiev. Physically he had survived the ordeal, but otherwise he had become a completely different man. Personal survival had become a top priority in his life, and all the fine qualities he possessed before had taken a back seat. While the Communist world was tearing him apart from outside, his own reactions were ripping him from inside. All along he knew that as a political prisoner he had compromised his conscience, which was purely dictated by the most primitive urge of self-preservation. Several times he had tried to justify his decisions through reasoning, but he knew he was merely trying to rationalize and make respectable a decision that was entirely self-serving. At that time he was so confused, he couldn't figure out with any clarity whether it was the lack of his own convictions or the mind-bending force of the warden that had changed the direction of his life. Anyway he had found the solution now. With very little left to salvage, he used the ultimate defense that God has given us all. He had neatly packed his world of emotions and stored it somewhere out of reach. He had built a strong shell around him and had retracted beneath it. At first his wife was able to creep under the shell, but soon he made it impermeable, effectively creating a world of his own. In the hospital where he worked, he gave his patients whatever he had to offer, which was becoming less and less. But that no longer concerned the State. In their eyes, he had become a rehabilitated Communist.

Then came the unexpected. He was sent to UNO to champion the Russian contribution to human dignity and freedom. He agonized for two full days in the hotel, where he was staying, in front of the United Nations Building. He knew if he let it slip by, this chance would probably never come back again. At the same time, he had no doubt how the Russians were going to react to this. On one side was a free world, where he had a chance to rediscover himself; on the other side was his wife, his culture, and his roots. Whatever decision he made, it had to be prompt, it had to be final, and above all, he must not fail. If he succeeded, he had to start all over again. If he failed, the rest of his life would be spent in Siberia. On the third day, the day before he was to go back to Moscow, he walked onto First Avenue. On this April day, the arrival of spring was simultaneously announced by the appearance of buds on the maple trees and the sudden multiplication of hot-dog stands on First Avenue. A calm wind was blowing from the river. People on the streets had a relaxed pace, for they were not intimidated by the cool breeze. At the traffic light, he turned right. The sun had suddenly burst through a conglomerate of clouds. Chimanski was free. He had abruptly entered the police precinct and asked for political asylum. The two KGB agents who had followed, continued ahead. They had their chance, but now it was too late.

But what he did not realize at that time was that this was not the end but just the beginning. In his first interview, his attorney in New York had stated that there was no way the Russians could prevent his wife from emigrating and going to the USA. As the money started running thin, the attorney scaled down his promises. The Russians played a typical game of mingling hope, dismay, and indifference. Finally, six months later, he got a letter from his wife. She had branded him a traitor and wanted a divorce. Chimanski knew these were not her true feelings, but what choice did he have? He accepted the divorce.

Lonely, but in a free world, which was so different to him, he plunged himself into his profession and entered into a surgical residency. Not that he liked surgery, but he knew surgery was going to demand maximum attention. That would keep his mind off matters of his heart and would further reinforce the steel wall he had built around his emotions. As the time went on, he completed the residency, started practicing in the same hospital, and found that his new world was absolutely compatible with his profession. Not only compatible, he found his new world predictable, not being influenced by emotional intrigues, for he knew he could not withstand another storm of his emotions. That only lasted until he met Judy Starsky. He remembered the first time he met her. He had just completed a difficult surgery, which was a matter of touch-and-go. As he walked out of the operating room, the nurse untied his gown.

"That was difficult surgery, Dr. Chimanski, wasn't it?" said Judy Starsky.

"It sure was." He threw his gown into the linen hamper.

As he turned around, Judy Starsky had just taken her mask off.

"I could see that in your eyes." Judy was looking straight at him.

"Nurse, let me give you a hint how to survive in the surgical world. Do not lose sleep unnecessarily over your patients."

Judy was still looking into his eyes. "I don't believe you, Dr. Chimanski."

"Why not?" he asked.

"Because you can pretend, but you cannot hide your concerns. They are written all over your face."

Chimanski kept looking at her as he walked away. A strange phenomenon had overtaken him. He could not define it, he could not describe it. Then a unique force penetrated the steel wall. An explosion had occurred within. Strange feelings surged inside him, which guided him to the nucleus deep inside him that had never been exposed before. It happened so fast. It was so precise. As he walked into the corridor of the hospital, he still felt Judy's incredible impact. It had infuriated him. He knew it was only a temporary event. He must put his life on the track again. He must get back to the world of medicine, which was more satisfying. As he entered the patient's room, he was back to his original form, or was he?

CHAPTER 3

Chimanski was right, for his patient had made an unbelievable recovery from surgery and after ten days had gone home. Medicine could not take the entire credit, for Jacobs exhibited an extreme degree of emotional stability and potential. He displayed an attitude as if negative forces had no place in his life. Chimanski had read Jacobs's success story in the press. Now, after meeting him, he knew why the man was immensely successful. A powerful thrust was pushing him forward and nothing could hold him back.

A strange mutual admiration had developed between the two, and the circumstantial acquaintance had evolved into informal friendship. Chimanski had never known a business tycoon before. Somehow, Jacobs did not fit into his image of a typical successful businessman, down-to-earth, pragmatic. Jacobs, on the other hand, displayed miscellaneous contradictions, idealistic yet unbelievably balanced. Partly inspired by his dynamic personality and partly because of the fact that it would not hurt to know a millionaire and an influential one too, Chimanski had fostered this friendship. As far as Jacobs was concerned, he did not need to seek any reason to like Chimanski. After all, he had saved his life. He was convinced that without a competent surgeon he would have died and his role on this earth gone unrecorded.

Chimanski was also perplexed regarding the whims of this rich man. Before Jacobs had gone home from the hospital, he had asked Chimanski if he would give a detailed description from the time he was shot until he regained consciousness. "Money would be no consideration," he told Chimanski. Inside, Chimanski was infuriated with the request. Strange people these are, he thought. They think everything is history. Their values are distorted. This man has paid no homage or thanks to the science that saved his life. On the other hand, he is going to spend money to recall an event that brought him to the doorsteps of science. Funny world. Crazy world. Instead of solving basic human problems, they are creating images. More monuments to their glory.

This February day Jacobs had invited Chimanski to spend the weekend with him in his country estate in central New York, in the Mohawk Valley. It was a bitterly cold February morning, the sort of cold that goes through the flesh and chills the bones, but even that wasn't enough to keep the New Yorkers off the streets. Jacobs walked into the Plaza apartments and took the elevator to the nineteenth floor.

"Stanley, pour yourself coffee. I will take a few minutes to get ready," Chimanski opened the door and led Jacobs to his living room.

"Another rough night?" asked Jacobs as he poured the coffee.

"Yes. Sort of. Did you hear the weather report? A fierce snow storm approaching from the coast," said Chimanski.

"I know, I called the airport. It will take three hours before it hits the airport. By that time, we will be near our destination."

Chimanski had just walked out of his bedroom. "Are you sure you don't want to cancel the trip?"

"No, no. It's only an hour's flight from here."

"You like to live dangerously, don't you?" asked Chimanski.

"Do you know that more people die from shoot-outs in New York in one week than from accidents in private planes all over the country in one year? If you want to get to a safe place, get out of New York, at least for a weekend."

Chimanski laughed, "I don't know which one to choose."

As Jacobs sat on the sofa in front of him on the table, there was an assortment of medical magazines.

"Don't tell me you read all these magazines."

"No, most of it is junk mail," said Chimanski. "Stanley, I will let you into a medical secret. Most of the physicians go through life practicing with a couple of dozen medicines. I am a surgeon. I will probably go through life with half a dozen."

"Incredible, isn't it?" although Jacobs did not look surprised.

"Yes, sir. Incredible, but true," said Chimanski.

Jacobs picked up a magazine with various organs displaying different colors. "Which damn tube was shattered in my body?" he asked.

Chimanski walked over, "Right here." He pointed to a broad red area in the middle of the body, "Aorta, they call it."

Chimanski walked back to the dressing table and started combing his hair.

Jacobs picked up a bunch of press cuttings and photographs from the table. "Look what my torn aorta has done for you." He waved the press cuttings.

"What?" Chimanski looked back.

"Made you famous overnight."

Chimanski smiled, "It certainly did. Although that's not the precise reason these are here."

Jacobs went through the press cuttings, "I must say you look impressive in the photographs."

Chimanski picked up his small suitcase. "All set. Ready to go. By the way, I would like to talk to you about these photographs sometime when you have time."

It was a clear sunny day. The small Cessna aircraft, with Jacobs in the pilot's seat, had completed its ascent. The tall geometrical Manhattan buildings, which appeared endless from the streets, from this height were stunted monsters, still abnormal but reduced to a proper size. The Cessna circled over the city, then crossed the Hudson River, and headed toward the Mohawk Valley. There was not a speck between the dark blue sky and the velvety white carpet covering the mountains and the valleys of the Catskills. Chimanski picked up the binoculars. There was a trail of confetti erupting from the mountain. A deer was running down the hill. Then the rising trail suddenly stopped. The deer had been shot by a hunter. Its antlers, sculptured gracefully,

plunged into the snow. It wasn't hunting season, but what difference did it make? Man had to be the master of this planet;
instant termination of life, his unquestionable right. Man, not
nature, must control the balance of wilderness.

Thirty-five minutes later, they landed at Oneida County
Airport. From there Jacobs piloted his two-seater helicopter.

Rising above the deafening sound of the chopper, he said,
"Easy from here. Just follow the Mohawk River eastwards."

Chimanski merely nodded.

In actuality the chopper was high enough, but it appeared
to be skimming the tree tops. Slabs of ice, sprinkled with flakes
of snow, stood stationary, choking the river. In some low-lying
areas, the slabs had overflowed the banks of the river and were
scattered among the surrounding fields. The sun had melted
and glazed the surface, and the ice slabs were now huge reflecting
mirrors.

The caretaker of the estate had cleared the snow, particularly
from the landing pad, which was clearly visible from the air.
Jacobs landed the helicopter.

A short man in his fifties, wearing a black-and-orange short
checkered coat and knee-high snowshoes, approached the
helicopter.

"Good afternoon, Mr. Jacobs," he said.

"Good afternoon, Mike. How are you?" Jacobs handed him
the small suitcases.

Mike disappeared into the house through the side door.

Chimanski and Jacobs walked to the front of the house. It
was on the east slope of the Mohawk Valley. They took a few
steps down toward the snow-covered lawn. Chimanski looked
at the rickety statue of Minerva, the Goddess of Wisdom. Over
the past sixty years, it had eroded and chipped from the fierce
snow and rainstorms. Its marble structure had lost its sheen,
but its greatest challenge was not from the natural disasters. It
was from man, a man named Charles Wells, who had owned
this property.

Master of his destiny at that time, he had an intuition for
the right investment. He had started a garment industry in this

area. Fueled by the cheap local labor and expanding New York's gluttony for fashion, his business had mushroomed into an empire. He had built this thirty-room house, complete with servants' quarters, surrounded by thirty acres of green land. Then came the thirties. The stock market crumbled. Banks collapsed. Some of his friends ended the agony by jumping from the rooftops. Others peddled apples from carts. But Charles Wells was a different breed. He was a fighter. He had taken hold of a hatchet and attacked the statue with the full force of his dwindling strength. The marble was hard, brittle, and slippery, but he wasn't going to give up. He was going to destroy this meaningless symbol, so he mustered all the strength he had and struck a devastating blow. The right arm of the statue fell on the grass.

There is a thin line separating sanity from insanity.

Chimanski looked at the house. It was a stone house built like a castle. Its walls were sturdy. There was a large white entrance. The narrow white windows were symmetrically and neatly arranged. He took a few steps down the landscape. The yews and mugo-pines on either side of the walkway were trimmed into globular and oval contours, with careful attention to details. Farther down, a blue spruce, more than thirty feet high, was trimmed into a conical shape.

Chimanski looked at Jacobs, more in resentment than surprise. Question was etched all over his face.

Jacobs smiled, "Yes. That spruce has been trimmed. . . . using a fireman's ladder."

"Why? You don't let them grow the way they are meant to?"

"No," he shook his head from side to side. "Undisciplined trees are like undisciplined people; they turn ugly."

That figures, thought Chimanski. Discipline was important. As vice-president of the biggest mineral-water plant in the world, how else could he run an organization that had ramifications in every nook and corner of this globe. Half a million employees spread all over. He believed in it and he instilled it. Discipline and loyalty. Expected from the corporate directors. Also expected from the bottom of the ladder, the Sea Cola peddlers. It wasn't so much a corporation; it was an international empire. Jacobs was the active king. It was all right to play the game according to the rules in America or Britain or France, but in countries of the Third World or behind the closed doors of Marxism the game was the same but the rules were different. The game was still to score more Sea Cola sales. The game might have to be played in the office of a dictator so that his coded Swiss bank account could be fattened or in the military barracks of a general who was about to declare a coup. Or in the bedroom of a Third-World leader who considered passion in addition to money as his fair price. All this to be carefully camouflaged, like wrinkles of an aging actress under the expertise of a cosmetician.

Jacobs looked appreciatively toward the house. "Would you believe? Bought it for forty grand in the spring of '80. Mind you, at that time, it looked like the Amazon jungle."

Yes indeed, at one time the Amazon jungle it was. After Charles Wells had moved to the Bronx, the house was unattended for forty years. Hay had replaced the lawn. It was growing as tall as the pussy willows. The bluish green Virginia junipers had lost their gentle character and were shooting for the skies. Rabbits and skunks had dug deep burrows. Local folks had seen ghosts around. One local farmer, who the villagers had suspected of being demented, had claimed that he had communicated with the ghost of Charles Wells. All this wasn't a waste. In '75 a restaurant was opened. The new owner had counted more on the ghost stories than the food to make his restaurant a success. He was going to attract people from the surrounding cities. He was going to satisfy their appetite with psychic phenomena rather than imaginative cuisine. He used to say, "Any crummy place can sell a steak for three dollars, but where on this earth would you find a decent ghost?" He was wrong. Two years later he folded his business. Stanley Jacobs had seen the advertisement in the *New York Times* and bought the house.

"See that dish?" Jacobs pointed out to large silvery dish antenna at the far end of the lawn. "It can pick up programs from every satellite that goes above. Let's go in. Have a drink."

The house was full of relics from all over the world. Chimanski poured himself a vodka to get the circulation going again in his fingers. He walked into the living room and looked out of the window. The west slope of the valley was gently curving, with the hills journeying toward the sky in a gentle and serene manner with a style of their own. On this clear day, farther away, the Cherry Valley hills, with their own distinctive blue tinge, unmistakably proclaimed their contribution to this spectacular view. Here the people, their machines, and nature lived in perfect harmony. The sun setting behind those hills, deprived of its fierce heat on this wintry day, looked like a large golden sphere that cast a mysterious spell, reassuring the whole co-existence without taking any sides.

Elsewhere nature had resented the people, and they had reacted in an infuriated manner, engaging in a conspiracy with their machines to devastate the challenging nature. In an effort to build monuments to their victory over the nature, the people had ruthlessly destroyed the oldest monument, nature itself, which, once destroyed, could not be reassembled, for the balance of its elements was so intricate. Not here though. Through mutual respect, which was so characteristic of the farmers in this area, they had overcome resentment of nature without actually destroying it.

"Stanley, you have a wonderful place here."

Said Jacobs, "Look at the beam over your head. It is etched on the beam that if there is heaven on earth, it's here."

Chimanski burst into laughter.

"I am not kidding. I etched it myself," insisted Jacobs.

Chimanski looked at the beam. "Are you a writer?"

"No. That I am not. I was visiting the Orient a couple of years ago, and I saw this centuries-old palace overlooking a river. They say at one time the walls of the palace were studded with diamonds. The English colonists took the diamonds out and replaced them with colored paint. On one wall is still written, 'If there is heaven on earth it is here, it is here.' When I look out of this window, I get the same feeling. Therefore, I etched the same message on my house."

Chimanski walked closer to the window as if to confirm the heavenly view. "It certainly is a tremendous view."

The Mohawk River was choked with slabs of ice produced by an unexpected thaw the previous week. The view of the river was partly obscured by leafless festoons of weeping willows and tall white birch trees stripped of their leaves. But the spruce trees, their character was tough. They stood there calmly, challenging the fiercest of the winds.

"Do you have any friends here?" asked Chimanski.

"No. I don't need them here. I have plenty of suckers in the city."

Chimanski's suspicions about this man were right. He was something else. On one hand, the man was bright, intelligent, and conniving. He probably deserved every bit of power and wealth he had. On the other hand, his unashamedly rich style was such a let-down. What a wastage. Such a sharp and conniving mind, instead of solving basic human problems, was channeled into selling more Sea Cola. The industrial world had doped and destroyed another brain, with the most intoxicating of all the known intoxicants, money itself. Chimanski thought money and power had become an addiction for Jacobs. The more he got, the more he wanted. His mind had been mottled and scarred by a thousand intrigues. His brain had followed innumerable lanes in pursuit of more wealth.

CHAPTER 4

Dr. Olig Chimanski had tried his best. He had tried persuasion. He had reasoned. But nothing worked. Finally in desperation, he took two weeks off and went out of the country. He needed time for the tornado within to settle down, so that he could return back to his original life, which had been calm and predictable. He thought it worked, but how wrong he was. When he came back from vacation, it started all over again. Finally, this evening, after an emergency appendectomy, his heart had completely overshadowed his sense of reasoning.

"Another life saved," he smiled at Judy Starsky. The depth of feeling in his voice betrayed that casual remark.

"I suppose so." Judy took her surgical mask off.

"It seems you do not believe lives are saved here," Chimanski wanted to keep the conversation rolling.

"Not always." She stripped her gloves off and rinsed her hands, to get rid of the powder sticking to her fingers.

"Is this remark meant for the medical profession as a whole or directed against a chosen few?" Chimanski was taken back at her curt remark. But tonight, whatever she said would have impressed Chimanski.

"If it is any consolation, you are not among them." Judy took her surgical gown off and thrust it into the soiled linen hamper. She looked at Chimanski. Her light blue eyes adjusted to a depth as if they knew their target within him. Her thin lips separated a little. Imperceptibly a smile appeared over them, which wasn't contrived but just meant to be there.

Chimanski wished he hadn't started this small talk. Life was going to get complicated. Judy, in the middle of all this, was going to get hurt the most. But he had no control over the events. A strange force had taken over his life. If he walked out of the place, a sickening vacuum would expand within him. If he asked her out, a huge phenomenon would engulf him. But he did not have to make the choice. He took a few steps toward Judy. "Would you have a drink with me?"

The smile had vanished from her face. Her blue eyes kept on invading inside Chimanski. A sensuous pink had appeared in her cheeks, which accentuated the color of her hair, which appeared like early spring hay that had just picked up its roots after devastating effects of a heavy snow, now washed clean with the first rainfall of the season, presenting a blend of gold and light yellow with a touch of orange. Her long, slender, body trembled a little.

"Yes, I will."

"I will meet you in the lobby," said Chimanski.

"All right. Give me twenty minutes," she said.

As Judy and Olig entered his apartment, she wasn't sure whether she was doing the right thing. She hesitated a little. After all, she was married. It was easy to start these things. Her infatuation with Chimanski was probably just that and nothing more. She was making the same old mistakes of building a fancy world around ugly realities. Where would it lead her? She and her husband were already drifting apart. This new friendship would only make things worse. It would push the wedge deeper and deeper between her and her husband.

Chimanski helped her take off her coat and put it in the closet.

"Judy, what would you like?"

"Whatever, Dr. Chimanski. Seven and seven." She walked over to the door leading to the balcony overlooking the East River. From the nineteenth floor, the two yachts looked like toy boats inching down the river.

"Please call me Olig." Tonight Chimanski's world was overwhelmed with emotion.

As he handed her the drink, her eyes surveyed him for a

moment or two and then they were lost in their own world. Chimanski gulped down straight vodka in a vain effort to calm his state of overcharged emotions.

She walked over to the sofa and sat down. She looked at the glass coffee table and tried to find a vacant space to place her drink among the scattered magazines and papers. She smiled. It wasn't a gesture of vanity. It merely reflected the state of the room.

Chimanski picked up the hint. "There are occasions when this room has looked better."

Her smile was mischievous now. "I agree. This room is certainly not suffering from terminal illness. I think it can be revived."

Chimanski burst into a brief laughter. He felt more at ease now. His guess had been right. Judy was not only unbelievably charming, she was also intelligent and quick-witted.

"How long have you lived in New York?" asked Chimanski.

"One year," said Judy.

"Do you like New York?"

In all honesty she could not have replied to that question with a simple no or yes. She hated New York. She was a small-town girl from New Hampshire. She hated this cold and inconsiderate city. But at the same time, she had met Chimanski who she liked and admired. Imperceptibly, a new dimension was appearing in her life.

"I suppose you get used to this place. Besides, it has its own rewards."

"What rewards?" asked Chimanski.

"Well, you meet a variety of people here who you would not expect to meet in a small place." She wished she had met Chimanski three years ago before she got married.

Chimanski poured himself another drink. "Two years ago I went to Maine for a short vacation. This was a small place. I suppose a couple of thousand people lived there. The only entertainment I found was watching Sears trucks go by."

Judy smiled. Inside she felt repulsed by the arrogance of the statement. But she knew Chimanski was right. For a man surrounded by plastic all his life, nature, as God meant it to be, can be very boring.

"So I guess you prefer the city life," she said.

Chimanski looked at Judy. If it weren't for her eyes, which exhibited kindness and concern with no element of intimidation, the rest of her appearance was so frighteningly aristocratic that developing a friendship with her would have been a prolonged task. But, then, one cannot match one's emotional make-up, which is dependent upon environment, with appearance, which is totally assigned by God. Perhaps there was no logic behind this matching game. Even if there was logic, it would not apply to Judy, for she was a unique person. He kept looking at her. How wrong he was. It wasn't her aristocratic face. It was her incredible beauty, as if a sculptor with all the time in the world had chiseled each feature to perfection. Her gently curving forehead, with slightly overhanging golden hair, stopping short of flair, but giving her, her own distinctive style. Her large blue eyes dissipated a strange mixture of concern and affection. Her long eye lashes, untouched by an artificiality, bestowed and endless depth to those eyes. Her cheeks had a firm yet smooth appearance, as if they had been given divine immortal blessing against any distortion. In that dim light of the table lamp, her thin wide lips, accentuated by the light lipstick she was wearing, appearing almost transparent. The sculptor had done a marvelous job.

"Do you like working in the operating room?" asked Chimanski.

"Surgeons fascinate me. Not so much the physicians. You people are unrealistic, rational, irrational, unpredictable."

Chimanski intercepted, "Sometimes bitchy too."

Judy laughed, "That's a nice drink. Yes, sir, that too. Some of you imagine that God makes drastic decisions only after consulting you."

Chimanski found that characterization of surgeons interesting.

"But that is understandable," continued Judy.

Chimanski smiled a little. "You mean there is a valid explanation of our bursts of insanity?"

"You do not need any explanation, Olig. I have never seen you hitting the roof. Others probably have their own reasons."

"Did you ever study psychology?" smiled Chimanski.

Judy just smiled. "Some surgeons feel they are superior human beings and treat everyone else like they should be treated, like particles of dust. Others have unhappy home lives, and the operating room is a good place to vent out anger because no one dares talk back to them. There is another category, which is inadequate surgeons. When surgery is not progressing as they've planned, they naturally throw the blame around."

Chimanski rubbed his forehead with his hand from side to side, "I don't believe it. I am getting free psychiatric help. Have you figured out my problem?"

"Not yet." She kept on looking at him. That magical depth had reappeared in her eyes. The room was pulsating with mysterious energy.

There was a ring on the phone. Chimanski reached for the phone, "They are always calling me at the wrong time."

Every day a drama of climax and anti-climax was being played in her life. Climax in the operating room. Anti-climax at home. As she drifted away from her husband, the operating-room work became a fascinating life for her. Surprises, aggravations, medical dilemmas being witnessed every day. Life-and-death dramas being played out in an atmosphere of casualness and seriousness, which was sometimes so difficult to tell apart. Here sometimes science contradicted religion, sometimes outright defied it, sometimes begged of it. Everyone there looked to surgeons for answers, knowing well that was asking for too much. Surgeons pretended to know all, mostly getting guidance from a very imperfect science, sometimes drawing strength from belief in God, but when neither came to their rescue, there was in their eyes, the deep, deep gloom of a little girl who has lost her favorite doll. Then they tore their masks off. Underneath was another mask that covered their frustrations and their broken pride. Judy always wanted to be and was part of that inner surgeon. She thought that is where she got closer to soul of a man. That was missing at home.

His fantasies, his hopes, and his lusts had all merged into

a cosmic phenomenon that defied all prescribed laws on this earth. The world around him had ceased to exist. Heavenly forces had taken over guiding his destiny. He had drifted to a remote place so far away, yet so familiar.

Judy looked into his eyes. She could not pretend any more. She felt a strange ecstasy, electrifying her entire body as if her whole previous existence had been preparing for this moment. If there was any doubt in her mind, it was expelled tonight. A thousand gods had descended into that room. They were telling her that it was not infatuation. It wasn't infidelity. It had nothing to do with the man-made rules. This was a different union. Two people who had wandered in the universe of souls, where time had no meaning, had finally found each other and were ready to merge. The air in the room was transformed into a living phenomenon, pulsating, and vibrant, responding to the irresistible pull between the two hearts.

He put the phone down and took a few steps toward her. He and she and the celestial force in the room had merged into one mass. He put his arms around her and kissed her gently. She was clinging to him as if her own separate existence had become a threat to herself.

"Judy, I know I have searched for you for a million years. I know we are destined for each other," he said.

"I know we are. It's so strange. I am not afraid of anything any more. Olig, I have peeped into your soul. All I need in life 's there."

It wasn't love. It was a different phenomenon. From now onwards their course and destiny would be charted by the gods. Nothing, absolutely nothing, could pull them apart. Love had pretensions. This phenomenon was so pure. Love had intrigues, this was so simple. Love had extrinsic forces, this was inner merging of two souls. It was an abstract phenomenon that exuded ecstasy not from physical contact but from intermingling of something undefinable. What flowed from it was a strange extract, which was simple, pure, and so priceless that it required no cosmetics or dressings to make it presentable.

Judy got up at five o'clock in the morning. The room was

filled with a strange blend of tranquility, excitement, and ecstasy. While the world around her was frantically moving in all directions to plunder the fruits of love, she had taken a step back and discovered a new dimension of life, not based on intrigues, artificialities, or lusts, but pure simplicity. The world had a different meaning for her now. She could not only taste the fun of life but also share in his agonies, which after all, life was all about.

Chimanski was still fast asleep. She touched him. Could he be crooked like the rest of the world? Couldn't be. He was tender and considerate, all effectively shielded behind a mostly gentle but sometimes defiant exterior. Chimanski, like other doctors, had a simple philosophy to aggressively treat a patient till he reached the point of no return. Judy thought Chimanski had an excellent instinct for judging that point of no return. This couldn't be said of some of the other doctors.

She distinctly remembered it was only last week when an eighty-five–year–old man was admitted with a bleeding stomach ulcer. The man was almost dead when he arrived at the hospital. The doctors used every artificial means, including ten units of blood, to revive him. Next morning there was a triumphant gleam in their eyes. Now he had blood pressure. Barely had he regained consciousness when the doctors decided there was no point in reviving him further and let him die peacefully, giving him morphine every two hours. The man died two days later. It would have been almost comical if it weren't for the fact that human life was involved. It was as if those doctors accepted the scientific challenge when the man was brought to the hospital, but as soon as the challenge was over, the scientific mini-gods didn't know what to do with him. This was a dubious application of science of medicine. Not so much to do with the patient, it was all about the scientific pride of the doctors. To them, medicine had become a tool to boost their ego. Judy knew Chimanski would never fall into that scientific trap. He had a sharp focus on his patients. Everything else, including science, God, and religion, only existed to sharpen that focus.

Judy reluctantly got out of bed. She could have lain endlessly in Chimanski's arms. The ecstatic moments still lingered in her mind. She could feel his firm body, his tight arms, and his lips. Now the world had a different meaning for her.

She went to the kitchen and put the kettle on the burner. She tried to figure out where she had been and where she was going in life. Madly in love three years ago, she thought she had found everything in the man she married. But by the end of the first year, the magic effect of the infatuation was fast disappearing. Her husband had taken off the mask by the end of the second year. He had become obsessed with his own inferiority. Judy's depth of perception and intelligence had intimidated him. In retaliation, he had treated Judy like a child treats a toy, to be played around and enjoyed and then, when enough is enough, to be kicked and ignored. Af first Judy protested. Then she resented and finally gave up. Now she knew how shallow her husband was. Her infatuation had built a smoke screen around him through which she could not see the real man. When the smoke slowly dwindled away, the naked realities surfaced.

She made herself a cup of instant coffee. As she sipped the coffee, she remembered she had been only six years old when her grandmother gave her a painted egg on Easter day. She still vividly remembered those blue and orange and green colors. The grandmother had brought her Ukrainian culture with her. She must have spent at least a day in painting that egg. The three-dimensional effect was so vivid she thought those painted figures existed in depth. Sooner than expected, certainly sooner than her grandmother expected, the egg rolled off the table and shattered into a hundred pieces. Along with that vanished her fantasies of those figures. She had believed that those painted figures existed in depth. But inside that egg was nothingness, an empty space. She had known her husband for four years. During the first two years, she had painted layers and layers of fantasies. During the third year, the shell had cracked. Inside was a vacuum, which was so different from the imaginary world she had projected outside the shell. The last year she had spent living in that vacuum. But that was past now. Chimanski was different. For a moment she thought she was making the same old mistake. No, it couldn't be. She had looked inside him. There were layers and layers of compassion surrounding his soul. If Chimanski was a farce, nothing else was true in this world.

As she turned the water on in the shower, she thought how interesting it was that God have given her everything a girl needed, beauty, perception, compassion, all conceived in endless depth, but fate had different designs for her. All her attributes had been blocked by the man she married. But now the game had changed. Her destiny had taken over her life. Not only the forces outside her control were steering her life, she was drifting without any effort in the right direction. As she turned off the shower, she heard a sound in the room.

Chimanski must be up, she thought.

She raised her voice, "Olig, did you say something?"

There was no reply.

"Olig, please give me a towel."

Fate certainly had different designs for her.

CHAPTER 5

At 9:00 A.M., a burly man walked toward the elevator across the lobby of the Plaza Apartments. He was a man in his fifties with considerable dimension of his abdomen, which overshadowed everything else he had. Except for a thin rim of hair at the back of the head, he was completely bald. His large brown eyes were bulging with a constant stare. He had a thick mustache, which made a right angle at each end of his mouth, but some of the hair, in blatant defiance of the rigid personality of this man, continued straight ahead. He came out of the elevator on the nineteenth floor. The policeman standing there took his hat off, just out of respect.

"Good morning, Inspector Drake," said the policeman.

Inspector Drake kept on his tumbling motion toward apartment number 24. As he walked, it was difficult to guess his center of gravity. It seemed the man was going to topple over any second, but that was only an illusion. He was well in control over his mind and body, certainly his mind. He, undoubtedly, had his share of bad luck. The last crime he investigated, he fell into so many pitholes that when he finally emerged with an answer, his pride had been bruised all around. Although, in essence, for Drake this was an open-and-shut case, this time he wasn't going to be misled into any traps. He was going to scrutinize from a completely detached perspective and look beyond the obvious for answers, which, after all, he thought, was the hallmark of a good detective.

While the detectives were going over the apartment thoroughly, taking photographs and lifting fingerprints, Inspector Drake in his own mind was reconstructing the crime, stopping every so often to search for the motive. But deep inside, he felt, from what he had heard, that it was only an exercise, for he knew the perpetrator of the crime. He was going to nail the bastard as soon as he had collected enough evidence.

He walked over to the front door, ignoring everything else he saw, for he realized that a prejudiced mind was going to be his greatest enemy. He looked at the front door. There was a deadbolt lock, which could only be opened with a key. He looked at the outside of the door. There was no evidence of forced entry. There were a few scratches and dents at the bottom part of the door. These marks obviously came from the shoes of the tenant pushing the door open while turning the key. His wife had found him guilty of the same crime several times at home. He went into the living room.

Detective Picciarelli was talking with a woman sitting on the sofa. He walked over to the door leading to the terrace. As he looked up and down, he saw a series of terraces stacked one above the other. There was always a possibility that the assailant could have come down the terraces, but that appeared highly unlikely. Still, he knew that was significant information. He filed it away somewhere in a remote alley of his brain, to be retrieved only if things start falling apart. He looked around the living room. Except for a few scattered magazines, everything else was in reasonable order.

He went into the bedroom. The dead body of Chimanski was lying on its side. There was dullness in his eyes. Blood on the pillow had formed a crust. Drake bent down to look carefully at the bullet mark. "Thirty-eight gunshot," he said to himself. There were tiny gunpowder marks around the bullet wound. Some of them were obscured by the small encrusted streams of blood. "Obviously shot from a very close range." Drake went around the room, pulling the drawers of the furniture. He found nothing disturbed. He went back to the bed again and looked for any signs of struggle, any undue wrinkling of the bed linen. He looked at the hands carefully. They were not clenching anything. He looked under the nails. No blood under them. The alarm was set at 7:00 A.M. He knew once this was analysed, he would know whether the death occurred before or after 7:00 A.M.

The next question was whether the murderer surprised Chimanski in bed or whether he opened the door and let him in. If Chimanski opened the door, he must have known the murderer. The other logical alternative was that the man had the key to the door and slipped in. Drake sat on the chair next to the dead body, trying to figure out how to eliminate all but one of these possibilities.

As he looked down, he saw a pair of slippers lying on the carpet near the right side of the bed. He kept on looking at them. The slippers were lying neatly on the carpet, with the toes pointing away from the bed. Supposing the bell had rung. Chimanski opens the door. The murderer walks in and pulls the gun, forcing Chimanski into his bedroom. The shortest distance between the door and the bed is the left side and not the right side. And besides, under such circumstances, either Chimanski would be wearing the slippers or they would be lying haphazardly on the left side. The fact that the slippers were neatly arranged on the right side led to the logical conclusion that the murderer had surprised him in bed.

Drake went to the window, opened it, and took a deep breath of the cold crisp air. Soon he shut the window, for he knew his lungs, which had been considerably destroyed by heavy smoking and the pollution of New York, could not stand more than a whiff of that chilled air. He lit a cigarette. He had temporarily relaxed his mind, for everything was falling into place. After he finished the cigarette, he went to the bathroom, looked around, and found nothing unusual. He went back into the living room. "Another senseless damn murder." For Drake this was the finest hour. His name would be flashed all over New York. He tried to hide his excitement by tight lips and a slight drop at each end of the mouth. But that was a poor performance. Eyes, which are such a reflection of mind, betrayed him. There in his eyes was that gleam, an unquestionable reflection of impending success. A surgeon who was in the news recently shot to death, the only witness to the murder was sitting there.

He knew this was the perfect juicy story. As he got closer to the third angle of the triangle, it was going to get juicier. The press was going to hound him, for they had to satisfy the public's insatiable appetite for this sort of stuff. It was anybody's guess who would be in the middle of all this commotion. Of course, none other than Inspector Drake. He would be charting the course of action. He would be in charge of press releases. With proper planning he could elevate his esteem and career to new heights. This time he wasn't going to stumble into any traps.

He noticed the woman, who was hysterical earlier, had somewhat calmed down now. His assistant, John Picciarelli, who was always at his best with women, had in his own way consoled her. Now the ungrateful task of asking probing questions was left to him. But he enjoyed it. The groundwork had already been laid. There was no point in delaying any further. Besides, unquestionably, one must hit the iron when it is still hot. Murder had been committed in this apartment, and the only witness was sitting there. Before she talked to her attorney and the truth got distorted, he had to move in with probing questions.

"Madam, I am sorry. I understand what you are going through," said Drake softly.

Nobody could understand what she was going through. How could a detective, who was after logic and motives, understand such an abstract phenomenon as love. A force greater than lightning had briefly illuminated her life. Now it was pitch dark again. Tears started streaming down her cheeks. Picciarelli handed her a box of Kleenex.

"Can I get you a drink?" asked Drake.

"No, thanks," she said.

"May I ask you some questions?"

She wiped her eyes in vain, for the continuous stream was still pouring down. No answer meant consent as far as Drake was concerned.

"Dr. Chimanski was shot twice in the head. Who shot him?" Inspector Drake sipped water from a paper cup. He would have preferred a martini.

"I don't know, Inspector."

Judy Starsky was somewhat more composed now. Her eyes had lost that magical depth. She was dejected. Everything around seemed insipid.

"Did you hear any shots?" asked Drake.

"No, sir."

"Mrs. Starsky, did you spend the night in this apartment?"

"Yes, I did." She was embarrassed and lost her eye contact with the inspector.

"Did you leave this apartment since you came here with Dr. Chimanski at ten o'clock last night?"

"No, sir."

"I know you are in a state of shock now." Drake knew the time had come to change his color like an iguana. "Mrs. Starsky, you have been in this apartment since 10:00 P.M. At 7:15 A.M. this morning, the Fourteenth Police Precinct gets a telephone call. Someone hears shots in the corridor and calls the police. Seven minutes later the police arrive and find Dr. Chimanski dead, and you expect me to believe that you never heard a sound?"

"I was in the shower." Judy started to cry, "I came out and found him dead."

That was the best news that Drake had heard all morning. Imagine telling this to the jury. They would laugh their heads off. With this sort of witness, he could twist the jury around his little finger.

Drake stook up and lit a cigarette. The drooping sides of his mouth had straightened out. *Who the hell does she think she it? Who the hell is she trying to protect?*

"Mrs. Starsky, we are not talking about toy guns. We are talking about .38 caliber guns. When you fire a .38, you hear a thunder a hundred feet away. I can assure you if you wanted to hear, you could have heard it even in the shower."

Drake hoped that Judy would pick up the sarcasm hidden in the statement, break down under the implied intimidation, and tell him the truth. Now he knew the motive and the murderer. The only thing left was a game of wits so that when he went to the courts, his task would be easy.

The tears in her eyes had dried. From Drake's tone it appeared tht she had been accused of conspiracy. Her problems had compounded.

"Inspector, I didn't hear any shots." She looked at Picciarelli instead. She thought he was more understanding.

"Mrs. Starsky, please try and concentrate. Did you hear any disturbance at all?" persisted Drake.

Judy shook her head from side to side. "No, Inspector."

"I only hope that you realize what you are saying." Drake felt time had come to change color again. "We are here to help you, but we can only help if you tell the truth. Those who knowingly hide the truth are accomplices to the crime and that, by itself, is a major crime. So I ask you for the last time, who killed the doctor?"

Drake couldn't care less what the hell happened to her. He was only interested in finding the last important missing piece of the jigsaw puzzle. Sitting there sobbing, with those big tears flowing down, they all looked innocent. You couldn't blame her husband. After all, the doctor was fooling around with his wife. They call it love. Anyway, who was he to pass judgment on morality? He was there to solve a murder.

Drake looked at Picciarelli and nodded. Piciarelli picked up the hint. Drake walked toward the door leading to the porch. Picciarelli continued the questioning. "Do you know where your husband was last night?"

"Business trip to Bridgeport, Connecticut." Judy felt more at ease with Picciarelli. He seemed to be more considerate and understanding. Unlike Drake, his eyes lacked the probing character. They reflected compassion and understanding.

"When is he expected back?"

"In the afternoon."

"Well, as a matter of fact, we found him in his office, Mrs. Starsky."

Judy discovered that Picciarelli's smooth appearance was equally deceptive. She had misjudged him. He was also laying a trap around her.

"I don't know; he told me he wouldn't be back until this afternoon," she explained.

"Does he know that you were friendly with Dr. Chimanski?"

"No. This is the second time we were alone together."

She didn't need to tell him she was in love with Chimanski. These two robots would not understand that you do not need to know a person for a million years to love him. To them, everything had to be explained by logic. There was no logic in her love for Chimanski, as there was no logic in his death. There was one thing certain now. Forever, there was going to be an emptiness in her life. Her life was going to be devoid of any meaning. Why should anyone kill a fine man like Chimanski? If there was logic in his death, only the heavens knew.

Drake realized Picciarelli wasn't getting anywhere with his questioning. He walked back and sat on the chair next to Judy Starsky.

"Mrs. Starsky, the police took seven minutes to come here. When you found the doctor injured, you never called the police, ambulance, or anyone else," said Drake.

"I came out of the bathroom and found Dr. Chimanski injured. He had no carotid pulse. I ran out of the apartment into the corridor to get some help. There I saw the police rushing in. With the help of the police, I tried to resuscitate him. It was too late."

"If you were frantically running out to get some help, why were you carrying your pocketbook?" Drake was eagerly waiting to see how she was going to get out of this mudhole.

"Was I?" She hesitated.

"Yes, Ma'am, two police officers saw you with the pocketbook."

"I remember now. When I came out of the bathroom, I thought Dr. Chimanski was still asleep. I had gone to his room to say good-bye."

Drake wasn't going to give up. "Just like you had forgotten why you were carrying your pocketbook, maybe now you remember who killed the doctor."

"Inspector, I didn't hear any shots. There was no other person in the room."

"Mrs. Starsky, someone pumped two bullets into the doctor. We detectives do not believe in ghosts." He handed out his business card. "There are a lot of unanswered questions. If you remember anything more, please call me right away. Detective Picciarelli will drive you to your home."

Inspector Drake came out of the apartment. At eleven o'clock there were no clouds in the sky. Still, the sun was unable to take the biting chill out of the air. He waited for a taxi. They were all occupied. Sons of bitches were busy carrying Arab shieks to and fro from the Waldorf Astoria. Finally a taxi stopped and drove him to the police precinct. As he entered the precinct, he realized he had nothing since his morning coffee. His physician, who had been treating him for hypertension, had insisted that he lose weight. Inspector Drake pleaded with the doctor that it must be the air or the water in his body that kept him overweight. But the doctor would not listen. He had taken Drake off all starchy and fatty foods, which were his favorites. Right now, Drake was famished beyond desperation. Questioning that bitch wasn't easy. He dashed out of the police station to the opposite bakery shop. Today, he deserved a large danish.

The police sergeant had dug up some information for him.

"Where is this woman's husband?" Drake poured himself coffee.

"Next room, Inspector," said the sergeant.

"Leave him there. Let him sweat for a while. Maybe he wants a cup of coffee."

The police sergeant told Drake that Chimanski had immigrated from Russia eight years earlier. For the first year, he had been under the surveillance of the FBI, but they had cleared him long ago. That didn't mean anything to Drake, for half the criminals on the streets of New York had been cleared by the FBI. "The social contacts of the doctor were almost non-existent. He was sort of a loner," said the sergeant.

Drake was losing his patience with the sergeant. "Who the hell cares where he was born? How long has he known this woman Starsky?"

"No one at the hospital knew they were friends," said the sergeant.

"What sort of doctor was he?" asked Drake.

"Surgeon."

Drake was more alert now. The danish had ultimately entered his bloodstream.

"Same doctor who operated on the vice-president of the Sea Cola, who was shot a couple of months ago?" asked Drake.

"Yes, sir, absolutely."

"I met this doctor when I was investigating Jacobs's shooting. How about this woman, what's her name?"

"Judy Starsky. Nurse at the hospital. Came to New York from New Hampshire about a year ago. Small-town girl, you know."

"How long have they known each other?"

"No one knows. If they do know, they are not talking. Her husband is so bitter about the whole thing, he cannot look beyond his wife's infidelity."

"All right, Sergeant, give me fifteen minutes."

The sergeant walked out of Drake's office.

John and Judy had been married for three years. By the end of the first year, they had begun to drift apart. The gulf between the two had widened, the energy for this destructive force being provided by their diagonally opposite needs, which each considered sacred. John Starsky had tried to change, but it was an effort. His marriage had become a smoke screen. Beyond that screen he was hiding his true love, which made him feel like a complete person. Judy to him was like any other object of art, an object with extreme beauty but one that still could not compete with his love. But today, in spite of all this, he had made a definite decision. He had opted for stability in life. No one, no one except Judy, could give him that. He knew while he was orientating his priorities in life, Judy was going to lead him in the right direction. She had the compassion. She had the understanding. Not now, of course. He had to wait until she recovered from the loss of her friend Chimanski. From that moment onward, his life was going to be an open book, not marred by deceit or dubious temptations. Straight life the way Judy wanted it, the way society wants it. The demons had tempted him to the other side of the hill. He had seen it. There was nothing but illusion there.

The sergeant walked back into Drake's office.

"Inspector, are you ready now?"

"What's your gut feeling?" asked Drake.

"I think he's your man," said the sergeant.

"Okay, why don't you roll him in? You cannot depend upon gut feeling; you've got to convert it into hard evidence."

John Starsky was in his late twenties. He had black greasy hair combed backwards, giving his forehead an unusually white appearance, his black beady eyes expressing contempt and indignation.

"Mr. Starsky, have a seat. Can I get you some coffee?"

"No thanks. How is my wife?"

"She is fine. Shaken up but okay," said Drake. "You know Dr. Chimanski is dead."

"So I understand, but I am not sorry." His beady eyes narrowed to a dot.

"Did you know him?" Drake lit a cigarette.

"No, I never met that scum." Contempt in his eyes had multiplied.

"How long have you known that he and your wife were friends?"

"I never knew that until this morning. Looking back our marriage has been falling apart for the past year."

"Sir, where were you last night?" asked Drake.

Starsky, who up to now had been talking with constant eye contact, looked toward the floor. "I was with a friend."

"His name, sir?"

"What's going on here? Am I a suspect?" retorted Starsky.

"No sir, this is just routine. Please write his name and telephone number." He handed him a paper and pen.

Starsky wrote the information on the paper.

Drake secured it and handed it over to Picciarelli, who had just joined them.

"It was my understanding that you had gone to Bridgeport,

Connecticut, on a business trip," said Drake firmly.

"Who told you that?" Starsky was visibly annoyed and wished that he had not been so cooperative with the detective.

Drake ignored that inquiry. "Sir, you haven't answered my question. Were you in Bridgeport or were with a friend in New York?"

Starsky stood up and banged his fist on the table. "What the hell does it matter where I was? What has that to do with that quack's death?"

Inspector Drake had glued his eyes on Starsky. "Sir, have you an alibi?"

"Are you crazy? Where do I find an alibi at seven in the morning?"

Drake knew he had got him now. "How did you know the doctor died at seven?"

"You said it, didn't you, or someone said it here."

"Let me warn you, Mr. Starsky. You have the right to remain silent. Anything you say can and will be used against you in a court of law. You have the right to talk to a lawyer or have him present with you while you are being questioned. If you cannot afford a lawyer, one will be appointed to represent you before any questioning, if you wish. You can decide any time to exercise these rights and not answer any questions or make any statements," said Picciarelli.

"Inspector, up to now I have shown an unusual degree of cooperation. I am not saying anything more until I consult my attorney."

Starsky got up and walked toward the door.

Drake, had to give his last professional touch, "Sir, I wouldn't leave the city for a couple of weeks. I will have lots of questions for you. Of course, along with your attorney."

CHAPTER 6

By 9:00 P.M., John Starsky had finished his third Bloody Mary in his favorite bar. He had turned the clock back. He was replaying his life, trying to figure out what had gone wrong. He still loved his wife. There was no denial that there were times when he felt repulsed by her ways. But that was no one's fault. She had an unrealistic philosophical view of life and perhaps that's why she had been attracted to that quack. He had never met the doctor, but that made no difference. They were all plastic people, highly polished and glittering from outside, but hiding filth within. They had no qualms about immoral acts. They justified and made their own standards. He was glad it was all over now. He was not going to lose any sleep over the loss of such filth.

He, also, had been deflected from the norms of life. Guilt had ridden his conscience ever since. But his problem was different. He could not help it. He was made differently. He had cheated on his wife, but that wasn't his fault. He was dragged away from her by an irresistible pull over which he had no control.

What about her? Would she ever come back to him in the real sense or would their lives drift apart endlessly in different directions? Right now there was nothing he could do. If he told her the facts, it would only add fuel to the fire and their relationship would be destroyed forever. He was willing to go to a psychiatrist. His problem was probably temporary insanity. But would Judy wait for him while he was getting help? Would she ever forgive him? But more than that, would she tolerate and understand while he was getting the treatment? The psychiatrist he had seen last month had told him that the treatment would not be easy. The tremendous gratification he had experienced in the past was going to be the main obstacle. But now things were different. It was going to be now or never. He could not afford to lose his wife. If Judy went, so did his sanity. With the doctor gone, things would be a little difficult for a while, but soon she would realize she could not live among the dead. If he changed now, they could get back together. On one side was stability in his life and everything else that went with it, on the other side was tremendous gratification. But he had made his choice. He had to get back to his stable life. And besides, he could reorientate his needs.

Tonight, in this bar, he was going to make a fresh start. The past was dead and the future was going to be bright so long as he played his game right. This time he was going to do it himself. He did not need the help of a shrink. He was not interested in the theories of unresolved Oedipus. He was not interested in analysing his past. He knew he had led a deviated life. He did not need to pay a hundred dollars an hour to hear what he already knew. He was going to rearrange his life and restructure his priorities, and that's all there was to it.

He felt the pressure of a hand on his left shoulder. He was glad Jim Bradley had come. For a while he was going to forget his worries and enjoy the man he admired and loved so much. He had been through hell since this morning. Now he could bare his soul open. After all, there were no secrets between him and Jim. Suddenly as if someone had opened a window and let in a gentle flow of spring air, he put his hand on Jim's hand and started caressing it.

"Jim, I need you. I am glad you came. I knew you would come."

To his surprise, he felt the fingers digging in his flesh. His thick jacket provided no protection against that grip. Jim had never been that rough before. He was always soft and delicate. But in their sumptuous relationship, he might have underestimated his strength.

Why is Jim so quiet today? He looked up. Jim wasn't there.

Instead there were two large black eyes focused on him. The squeeze on his shoulder was so strong that it was going to dig the bone out of the socket.

"I am sorry to disappoint you, Mr. Starsky. I think you remember me." The squeeze on the shoulder abated. The man sat on the stool next to him. He pulled a partly rusty badge out of his pocket and placed it in front of Starsky. "Inspector Drake from the Fourteenth Precinct. The man with me is Detective Picciarelli."

"I told you this morning, didn't I, that I would not answer any questions," replied Starsky.

The bartender looked at Drake, expecting an order for a drink. Drake flashed his badge at him. "None for me. Leave us alone for a minute."

Drake looked at the bartender, who, although he had moved a distance, was still trying to pick up the conversation.

"Mr. Starsky, you don't understand. I have no questions. I would like you to come with us."

"What for?" This time Starsky wasn't going to be pushed around by these two bluffs.

"Mr. Starsky, I'll give you a choice. Either you walk out of here quietly or I will drag you out of this place."

Starsky walked out of the bar accompanied by the detectives. Drake was holding Starsky's arm with his huge left hand and his right hand close to his gun in case the son-of-a-bitch got any ideas. Picciarelli drove the police cruiser. Drake sat with Starsky in the back seat. "Mr. Starsky, how long have you been in this bar?" asked Drake.

"Where are we going? Is my wife all right?" Starsky looked out of the window, trying to figure out which direction they were going. Drake kept on looking ahead.

"Why, do you think something could have happened to her?" asked Drake.

"Inspector, stop playing games with me. Where are you taking me?"

"All in good time, sir."

His mind raced through the dark crevices of his life. Had

they found angel dust hidden in the car? Not likely. It was securely hidden under the hood of his car, enclosed in an asbestos casing. Last week when Jim Bradley needed a quick fix, he had trouble locating it. But those police dogs. Damn sniffers. Police can't search his car without a warrant.

Surely they were taking him to the police station. Grass cigarettes in his pocket. Must get rid of them. As soon as they reached the station, the pigs were going to frisk him. It's a small miracle they hadn't already spread his legs.

He had only two left in his pocket. Two he had already smoked. But tonight they had a different effect on him. Normally, two was his limit. It was enough to slowly extricate him from the crude world of reality and implant him in a mindless world, a world without reason, without explanations, without pressures. Only emotions. But this evening he was still sad. He was still in turmoil.

His mind searched deeper. They probably got to Jim Bradley, busted his place and found the dust. It wouldn't take too much to break Jim. He was delicate and gentle, not used to third degrees by these brutes. It would have been different if he had been there to protect him. Jim wouldn't implicate him.

Had they been taking to Judy? Maybe he should have stayed at home. What did she tell them?

Everything that happened today was engulfed in a dense fog. He remembered being with her in the afternoon. Streams of tears had been flowing down her cheeks.

"Senseless murder. Why, God?" She was talking to the four walls.

His eyes were fixed on Judy. "Senseless?" He exploded into perpetual laughter. Then, almost abruptly, the laughter stopped. He sat on the bed by her side and put his arm around her. "Honey, I will make it up to you."

"John," she dried her tears, "it's all over between us."

"Just like that." He took a deep puff at his cigarette. "I tell you, that stinking corpse is all over. Rightly punished by God."

She covered her eyes. She wanted to be alone, alone in solitude, away from this ruthless world. She knew John wouldn't understand. She and Chimanski were intertwined forever. Death would not change that. Death might delay but never alter their destiny. She was sobbing, "I love him."

"Can't live amongst the dead, Judy, we have too much in common," said John.

"It's over. I don't want you to stay here tonight."

He stood up. He was shaking in anger. "No one tells me to leave."

"Then I'll go," she said calmly.

"You bitch. Don't you understand? We are in it together. Cops are out to nail me. All you see is that scum."

She stood up and put on her coat. "Decent man. He didn't deserve to die."

"Where the hell you think you are going?" He squeezed her face between trembling hands.

"I am not staying with you." Her eyes were calm, partially covered with smudged mascara. Her lips pressed together, indicating the firmness of the decision she made.

"You are not going to talk to the cops," he said, "until we have discussed it with our attorney."

"I have nothing to hide," she said.

The bull had seen the red cloth. He was ready to charge. Anger and frustration had overpowered him. With his hand he hit her again and again. When she fell down, he kicked her.

"A bitch in heat uses more discretion." His beady eyes were protruding. "Not you."

She didn't expect anyone to understand her love for Chimanski, and she didn't care. For a moment her body shuddered. Not so much in pain but in anguish. Then it was all over. She stopped crying. Suddenly it was calm and ecstatic. She was back with Chimanski. She knew he was right. They had searched for each other for a hundred, perhaps a million years. Death was a temporary event. Time was an illusion. Chimanski would never let her go again. They had both discovered a new meaning of love. Not her husband, not Chimanski's death would separate them. Maybe she didn't have to wait any longer. Anyway in this cosmic phenomenon she had witnessed, time was meaningless.

John Starsky kneeled by her side. A lump, the size of a egg, had appeared on her right eye. He reached out to the bed and dragged a pillow and put it under her head. Her eyes were closed. He kissed her on the lips." I am sorry, honey." She heard nothing. She felt nothing. She was in a different world. He stroked her face gently and eased her hair away from her face. Then he went to the night stand and picked up the gun.

He crouched up in a corner, his eyes fixed on Judy. He checked the chamber of the gun. There were three bullets in there. All he needed was one. He knew the storm had been brewing up for a while. He had ignored the warning winds, and now gusts of immense ferocity were hitting him. There was total devastation. It would never be the same again. It was too late to pick up the pieces.

An hour later he was driving aimlessly through the Manhattan streets. The sun had been choked earlier than sunset time by the thick dark clouds. Darkness had shrouded the side streets of the city. He went into a telephone booth and dialed.

"Jim," he broke into loud sobs.

"Pull yourself together," said the firm yet delicate voice. Tears were flooding and choking the mouthpiece.

"Jimmy. You don't understand. I am finished."

"John. I understand. Hang on. I'll see you in the bar—say, an hour," said Jim Bradley.

"I need you now," he pleaded. His eyes, covered with tears, were transformed into plastic knobs reflecting the street light erratically.

"I'm sorry. Please understand."

"I will come to your office right now," said Starsky.

Jim Bradley had his briefcase in his hand. He was ready to leave when the phone had rung. This was his fourth year in practice as an attorney. He had dreams of becoming a high-powered criminal lawyer who would be defending and saving his clients with crucial evidence that had been overlooked by his peers. Or of a corporate lawyer defending successfully the breakdown of giant corporations. Reality had shattered those dreams. He was paying the rent by prolonging the settlement of divorce cases. And, thank God, there was no dearth of people slipping and tripping on New York streets and suing the owners for neglect.

"Not now. And I can't talk on the phone," said Bradley.

"But, Jim." He was in tears. "Want to be with you."

"Try and understand. Cops just left. They are sniffing around. Have to go home to clean up the dust."

Starsky was crying like a child whose mind was fixed on a lost toy.

"Damn it. I need you."

"Listen. I will take care of everything. See you in the bar at seven." Bradley put the phone down.

The cruiser stopped in front of a dull gray brick building. Drake pushed the bell button. Almost instantaneously a man looked at them through a small window in the door. He opened the door. They went through a narrow corridor, painted yellow, dimly lit with a single sixty-watt bulb, with crusts of paint peeling off. Drake pushed the swing door. The room was deathly cold, yet there was no movement of the air in the room. Drake looked at the thin pale man.

"Pull out number nineteen," he said.

He pulled the stretcher out a little and carefully read the tag tied to the big toe. Then he pulled it out of the freezer all the way. A blast of cold wind froze the already cold room. There was body wrapped in a white sheet. Gently, as if not to disturb it, the thin, pale man uncovered the face. Starsky took a step forward. Suddenly, a sickening heaviness filled his eyes. His vision blurred by the tears, he momentarily rubbed his eyes.

Her serene, ashen face with her eyes closed was throwing a peculiar philosophy into that room. "There was nothing, absolutely nothing that happens in vain in this world."

He held her face within both hands. His fingers were numb. He could barely feel her ice-cold cheeks. He opened her eyes. Dullness had appeared in them, partly obscuring their blue color. Blood had drained somewhere out of her cheeks. Drake was no judge of beautiful women, but he thought she had exquisite features. What a waste, he thought.

John Starsky's life and dreams were over. He walked out,

limped into the rear seat of the cruiser, and looked at Picciarelli.

"Who killed her?" he asked.

Picciarelli looked at Drake. He said nothing. Drake had his own game plan, and Picciarelli wasn't going to mess it up.

Drake sat by the side of Starsky. "Police station is only two blocks away."

God, why this had to happen to him, especially now. The doctor was out of the way. He had made up his mind to change. Judy would have gotten over his death in a couple weeks. He should not have left her alone today. Who killed her or did she commit suicide?

Drake and Starsky walked into the police station followed by Picciarelli. He poured a cup of coffee for Starsky and himself.

"Mr. Starsky, I am sorry," said Drake.

"Inspector, who killed her? How did she die?"

Drake had perched himself on the chair behind a large desk. Papers were scattered all over the table. The green vinyl covering on the table was ripped off in several places, with gray dirt permanently incorporated into the vinyl. Drake didn't care. He hated the enormous paperwork that accompanied every homicide. Drake lit a cigarette.

"I was hoping you will help us, sir," said Drake.

"Inspector, I don't want to play games any more. Have you informed her parents?"

"We thought it would be rather appropriate if you did that, unless you want us to," said Drake.

"I will take care of that," said Starsky.

"Do you think she could have committed suicide?" asked Picciarelli.

"No. She wouldn't. She loved her life too much. Hers as well as others," said Starsky.

"In desperation, all of us lose logic. Have you any idea who could have killed her?" asked Picciarelli.

"We have no enemies." Starsky's voice was barely audible.

Drake intervened, "It was no suicide. The bullet wound is in the back of the head."

"Inspector, this morning you suspected me, I can understand that."

Drake got up and closed the door completely so that there was no clatter of typewriters coming from outside. He stretched his legs under the table. He was going to feed information and give Starsky enough rope to hang himself.

"Mr. Starsky," said Picciarelli, "I have to warn you that you have the right to remain silent. Anything you say can and will be used against you in a court of law. You have the right to talk to a lawyer and have him present with you while you are being questioned. If you cannot afford to hire a lawyer, one will be appointed to defend you, before any questioning if you wish. You can decide at any time to exercise these rights and not answer any questions or make any statements."

Starsky did not resist. "I understand," he said.

Continued Picciarelli, "You understand each of these rights I have explained to you?"

Starsky nodded.

"Having these rights in mind, do you wish to talk to us now?"

"Yes, I do. I have nothing to hide."

"Do you have any idea who could have killed your wife," asked Drake.

"Inspector, she didn't have an enemy in the world."

"How about the doctor? Do you think he had an enemy in the world?" asked Drake.

Suddenly anger had appeared in Starsky's eyes. "I never knew that scum existed until this morning."

"Sir, where were you between five and seven this evening?" asked Drake.

"I went to see Jim Bradley."

"Did you have an argument with your wife before you left?"

"Yes, we did."

"Could you describe it in a little more detail?"

"Well, this morning, after I left the police station, I went home. She was upset and crying. I said something about her association with the doctor, and an argument broke out. One thing led to another. She asked me whether I had killed Chimanski. I knew she couldn't mean it. I was mad. There was a heated argument. I stormed out of the house at five o'clock to cool down."

"What was she doing when you left?"

"She was lying on the bed and crying. I left the house to cool down. I had no idea how to deal with this situation."

"So, where did you go?" asked Drake.

"I went to see Jim Bradley."

Drake smiled. "You mean you went to discuss your personal problems with him."

"Yes, we are very close."

"How close?" He fixed his eyes on Starsky.

"I wanted someone to talk to."

"So what did you talk about?" persisted Drake.

"I discussed the mess I was in. Even after what she had done to me, I still loved her."

"What did your friend say?"

"I don't know, I was so confused. What does it matter anyway? Who cares what he said? She never hurt a soul."

Drake took a fresh pack of cigarettes out from his pocket and offered one to Starsky.

"No, I don't smoke."

Drake's game plan was right on schedule, in fact, better than expected. Starsky was digging a deep hole and when it was deep enough, Drake was going to push the dirt and bury him. He looked at Picciarelli for a moment. Picciarelli marveled at how brilliantly and skillfully Drake was handling this, making sure every angle was covered.

"Mr. Starsky, do you take any drugs?" continued Drake.

"Certainly not."

"Have you ever smoked marijuana?"

"No. What has that to do with my wife's death?" he protested.

"Well, have you ever?" insisted Drake.

"Never."

"What happened afterwards? Where did you go after you left your friend?"

"I drove aimlessly for about an hour. After that, I went to the bar where you found me."

"Is that your favorite bar?"

"Yes."

A sparkle had appeared in Drake's dark eyes. His thick lips separated a little. He had managed to put the net around the fish. Now the time had come to tighten the net. He took a deep puff at his cigarette. Picciarelli, who was still learning the detective game, was churning acid in his stomach in anticipation of the finesse with which Drake was going to deliver the final blow. Drake had collected all the trump cards he needed. He was holding them back skillfully, while Starsky's cards were lying on the table. Drake and Picciarelli knew the game was over. Drake stook up from the chair and leaned forward on the table. For a second, he had lowered his voice almost to a whisper.

"I noticed there were no girls in the bar," said Drake.

Starsky could not look at Drake's eyes. He looked toward the floor. Drake walked over to the chair next to Starsky. "The fairy tale is over. The fairy has decided to leave the faggot's castle. I suggest you come out of the fairyland and tell us the truth."

"What do you mean, Inspector?" His eyes were still fixed on the floor.

"Let me put it this way. Your fairy, Jim Bradley, has decided to cooperate with the police. The evidence he shall give will put you in the slammer for life. I suggest for your own good that stop telling us tales and come out with the truth. The jury will understand revenge murders. The jury will understand passionate murders. But they will not understand the agonies of a fag."

"Jim wouldn't do that."

"Oh, yes, he would. All of you have fickle minds and that's how you get sucked into this disgusting life."

"Jim wouldn't. He is an honorable man."

"Well, let's see how honorable he is. I offered you a cigarette, you refused. I don't blame you because you are used to smoking grass. The night before Chimanski was murdered, you told your wife you were going to Bridgeport. But you know where you were. You were with your fairy, sniffing cocaine all night, smoking grass and all that crap that goes with it. We searched his apartment and found two ounces of cocaine." Drake smiled and continued, "He must love you, spending all that money on you." Drake stood up and walked back to the chair behind the desk. "But what good is the money if it cannot buy you pleasure?"

Starsky was rubbing his eyes. He could not control his tears. He was sobbing. He was banging his wrists on the table.

"Inspector, I was going to get help from a psychiatrist."

"Sir, it's not my place to say, but I will say it anyway. You did not need to go to a psychiatrist to tell you what was wrong. You are into drugs. You are into homosexuality. Then you wonder why your wife was fooling around elsewhere. Supposing you give us the murder weapon, the .38 caliber gun. Same weapon used on both victims."

Starsky said nothing. He was still sobbing.

"In the morning, I will talk to the district attorney. I cannot promise anything. If you cooperate, we can work out some arrangement. Sir, where is the gun?"

"I didn't kill anyone, and we did not have an enemy in the world."

Drake suddenly got up from his chair, walked around the desk, and sat on the table facing Starsky.

"Mr. Starsky, the time has come that you start playing another tune. I am running out of patience. Let me see where you stand. Dr. Chimanski died between six and seven this morning. You said you were with your friend, Jim Bradley. He will testify that you spent the night there, but what he will not testify is that you were with him between six and seven. You will understand, he was so much conked out by your fairy games and drugs that he does not remember a thing. So there goes your first alibi. You said you were with him between five and seven this evening. Absolute lie. Jim Bradley was making a deal with the district attorney at that time. Don't get me wrong. The man loves you. He cried too. He first chose to remain silent, but what broke the silent code of the homosexual were the two ounces of cocaine we found in his apartment. He knew that could put him behind bars for ten years. So he decided to cooperate with the police. You know where that leaves you? In the freezer."

Starsky knew Drake was right. He was standing in a deep gorge, all alone, with steep rocks on either side, which could come tumbling down any time. Who was to blame but himself? He had driven her from crisis to crisis and ultimately death. His abnormal association with Jim was doomed from the very beginning. That's not the way things were meant to be. He should have listened to the psychiatrist. He should have listened to his friends. Too late now.

"So you see, Faggy Face," said Drake, "you don't stand a chance. Your best bet is to come out in the open."

Starsky said nothing.

"Mr. Starsky, you are under arrest. You have until 9:00 A.M. to make up your mind. If you tell the truth, I will talk to the district attorney. If you do not, I will throw the book at you. I will charge you with the first-degree murders of Dr. Chimanski and your wife."

Picciarelli untied his tie. He took him to the detention room next door. It had been an exhausting day for all of them.

Over the years Drake had learned one thing, and that was not to get emotionally involved with the problems of the victims and the suspects. After all, death and tragedy was a daily drama in his life. If he let emotions enter his life, logic would be the first casualty. Without logic, there could be no detection.

Picciarelli was different, but that was perhaps because he had not yet mastered the tricks of the trade. He liked to dwell on human aspects.

Drake poured another cup of coffee and lit a cigarette. "Picciarelli, tell you one thing. The day after the crime, all criminals look like the Twelve Apostles sitting at the Last Supper. So let us sit down and reconstruct the crime as I see it. You point out any fallacies in my theory."

"I think Starsky suspected all along that his wife had been

fooling around with the doctor. So he made up this little story about going to Bridgeport, but instead, he went to see his lover, Jim Bradley. There, he poured his guts out, in addition to everything else. Under the influence of drugs, he decided to pay an early visit to the doctor's apartment, where he knew his wife was. He went to the apartment. The doctor was still asleep. Judy opened the door. Some argument broke out and he shot the doctor in bed. Picciarelli, you will be the devil's advocate, won't you?"

Said Picciarelli, "Okay, how did he enter the apartment?" He wasn't sure whether that was an intelligent question or not.

"That's a very interesting question. Because if we can prove he had the key to the apartment, that makes it a premeditated murder. But if we can't, then I suppose we will have to pin a lesser charge on him. Although the very fact that he carried a gun to the apartment will, in my opinion, make it a premeditated murder, but that I will have to leave up to the district attorney. So, in answer to your question, my guess is that his wife could have opened the door rather than create a scene in the corridor of the building."

"Another flaw," said Picciarelli. "If both were conspiring, why did she say he had gone to Bridgeport, while he confessed that he was in his friend's house?"

A smile had appeared on Drake's face. "Well, that's where we scored. Before both husband and wife had time to discuss their versions, we moved in with probing questions. That's what I mean when I say we must strike while the iron's hot." Continued Drake, "By the way, did you notice how the bastard had to struggle to bring tears to his eyes when he discovered his wife had died and how he sobbed and let out a stream of tears at Jim Bradley's abandoning him. I can smell those damn fags from a distance."

Picciarelli was visibly annoyed, "Wait a minute. Any psychiatrist will tell you that you can't tell these people apart from common citizens, at least these days."

"Come on, Picciarelli, you don't believe those shrinks. They think everything is normal. This is how they make a living.

Anyway, so he shot the doctor. Somebody heard the shots in the corridor and called the police. I tell you, this nurse was a smart cookie. And why not? After all she worked in the operating room. They are trained to stay cool under pressure. She asked her husband to leave, then collected every single item that belonged to her, and tried to get out, leaving no trace behind."

Picciarelli took his tie off, which was hanging loosely around his neck. "It's interesting how no one, on either side of the apartment, heard the shots and how a guy walking in the corridor was able to exactly pinpoint the apartment in which the shots were fired."

"Well, Picciarelli, you have to understand the New York psychology. Here, no one wants to get involved. People don't want any hassle coming to the courts."

"Why did Judy wait five minutes before she tried to get out of the apartment?" asked Picciarelli.

"Well, that's obvious. She did not want to leave any evidence behind. You know she came out of the apartment with her pocketbook. Now you tell me, does that make sense any other way?"

Picciarelli was still persistent. "Talking to her, I had the gut feeling she was telling the truth."

"My dear boy, in police work, you do not depend upon gut logic; you depend upon brain logic. First, she didn't hear the shots. Second, she was going out of the apartment, leaving no trace behind. I think she was guilty as hell of conspiracy. Anyway, they go home. Some argument breaks out between them. She threatens to call the police, or he thinks she is going to tell the truth. Fickle as these fags are, he panics and shoots her in the back of the head. He was sure his fairy, Jim, would give the alibi, and he would have if we hadn't discovered the cocaine. Now she tried to reach me at 4:45 P.M. The message was she wanted to talk to me. At 5:30 P.M. I called her back. There was no reply. At 5:45 I reached her home and found her dead lying on the floor. There was no forced entry. Shot twice in the back of the head. Multiple bruises over the face.

"Wait a minute, Inspector Drake. You are forgetting the third angle of the triangle. Jim Bradley. Listen to this. According to the district attorney, Bradley told him that John Starsky called Jim at 4:00 P.M., telling him that their relationship was finished forever. This gives us a lead in a different direction Bradley could have gone into rage at the thought of Starsky leaving him and he probably did the only logical thing expected of an insane person, that is, eliminate the obstacle. I mean, he killed Judy Starsky."

Drake burst into perpetual laughter. When it was over, his face was beet red. "Picciarelli, you know what that means? If you can prove that, you can kill two fags with one stone. And that's precisely what my plan is. But I want to do it a little differently. I want to keep pressure on Starsky, while the district attorney is keeping pressure on Jim Bradley. If my intuition is right, soon they will be at each other's necks. And your and my job will be easier."

Said Picciarelli, "I see your point." He pulled a diary out of his pocket. "I have an autopsy report on Dr. Chimanski. Number .38 gun. Shot from a very close range. One interesting observation by the medical examiner. No gunpowder burn around the wound edge, although lot of powder sticking there."

Drake, who was resting his feet on the table, was instantaneously back on his feet again. "Don't tell me . . . let me guess. Dr. Kundra is the medical examiner."

"Right." Picciarelli was surprised. "How did you know?"

"Because Kundra likes to play 'Quincy.' Anyway, this powder business, what is that suppose to mean?"

"I asked him. He said he needs time to look under the microscope before he can give a definitive answer."

Drake had a mouthful of Milky Way chocolate. He swallowed it quicker than he would have liked to. "You lost me there. What the hell is he looking for?"

"I suppose he is looking for the powder burn," replied Picciarelli.

Drake slumped back into his chair. "I don't believe this. While you and me are dragging our asses all over the city to solve these murders, this son-of-a bitch is being paid fifty thousand dollars a year to look under a microscope. What the hell does it matter how deep the burn is? Can't he tell from the size of the wound how close he was shot from?"

Picciarelli lit his pipe.

Drake continued, "I don't care what he finds under the microscope. The facts are, one, no signs of struggle. No forced entry. Conclusion—assailant knew both victims. Two, both are shot in the back of the head from close range with the same weapon. Conclusion, one assailant who knew both victims. Three, lies from John Starsky. Conclusion—low credibility. Four, Starsky, confirmed homosexual—credibility zero.

Picciarelli put his pipe on the table. "I wish you wouldn't make such a big thing out of his homosexuality."

Drake was amazed. He raised his eyebrows. Somewhere on his thick lips, hidden behind his bushy mustache, a smile had appeared. "Why, Picciarelli, why does that bother you?"

Picciarelli got a little nervous. He picked up his pipe, started nibbling on it rather than puffing. "Not because of what you think. But you keep hammering at this, and the jury might think you are a prejudiced man."

"Do I get the feeling that you approve of these deviated characters?" said Drake.

"No, I certainly don't," said Picciarelli abruptly. "But I don't believe that by being homosexual, we can assume that his credibility is zero."

Drake wanted to get out of the argument. "Anyway, I have told you four facts. You look for a common denominator; the answer is John Starsky. Go and get some sleep tonight. Sharp nine in the morning, we will book this son-of-a-bitch."

CHAPTER 7

In spite of all predictions to the contrary, this was turning out to be the mildest March. As Inspector Drake walked out of the subway station at Fifth Avenue, he was surprised that he wasn't hit by the usual cold wind whipping down the entrance of the subway. Today the wind was cool and refreshing. The newsstand on the corner was full of customers snatching papers and cigarettes in a hurry. The Chinese man behind the counter displayed an uneasiness reflected in his roving eyes and constant clumsy movements of his fingers. He was trying to reassure himself that if the catastrophe struck again, he was ready for it. His stand had been hit by hold-ups twice in the past year. From his reactions, it looked as if the man was not about to give up. This time he had a loaded gun ready behind the counter, close to the cash register.

As Drake read the headlines, it seemed America was back on the track again. Unemployment was falling, and inflation had slowed down to 5 percent. Drake continued his leisurely pace down Fifth Avenue. He glanced at his watch. There was plenty of time. He looked in the window. Long dresses with big blue flowers on a yellow background must be the fashion this spring. He felt warm and took his coat off. As he reached Park Avenue, there were already flowers budding in the median. Spring was here. The sun was peeping through the crossing street. He went down Park Avenue for a couple of blocks and pushed the thick glass door of the Cafe Galaxy. He lit a cigarette and casually surveyed the small restaurant.

On this Sunday morning, the restaurant was practically deserted. In the far corner, there was a tall man sipping coffee. He had a broad forehead. His cheekbones were bold, raising a suspicion that somewhere in his family tree Indian blood might have got admixed. His face was pitted and scarred from burnt-out acne, the destructive ravages of which were more apparent on the right side, giving his face an asymmetrical appearance, particularly when he smiled. His dark red hair was brushed straight back. His steel gray eyes put a damper on his otherwise rough exterior. He had a long, expressionless face. His eyes were glued to the cup of coffee. As Drake got closer, he saw the man tapping the side of the cup in a rhythmic manner. As he got closer, he heard the tinkling sound generated by the rhythmic tap.

"Please sit down," said the man. "I am Jim Reeves."

"Inspector Drake." Drake sat opposite him.

The waiter approached the table.

Said Reeves, "Unusually warm day, isn't it?"

"Yes, it certainly is," smiled Drake.

The waiter poured coffee for both and left.

"I hope you didn't ask me to come here to discuss the weather," said Drake.

"Not quite. I would like to discuss something more important, like two murders in your city."

Asked Drake, "What do you want to know?"

"Everything."

"What do I get in return?"

"What do you have in mind?" asked Reeves.

"I know you FBI guys. I am sure you have dug up some skeletons. Supposing we pool our information. That will be a decent thing to do," said Drake.

Reeves was gently tapping his knuckles on the table. "I haven't come here to barter. We think a federal crime has been committed, and you can help us."

"I don't think there is a thing wrong with that. At the same time, two people have been murdered in the core of the Big Apple. If you have any information, I am entitled to see it."

"Mr. Drake, you know the name of the game. I am sure the

commissioner of the police has discussed this with you," said the FBI agent.

Drake was annoyed. "Yes, indeed he has. I also know why. He pisses in his pants the moment he gets an FBI call. You people can make a national security issue out of anything you like. Anyway, how did the FBI get involved with this?"

"Well, we are not really involved. We just want to make sure a federal crime has not been committed."

"Go on," said Drake.

"Well, the fact of the matter is that Mr. Williams, the president of the Sea Cola Corporation, has complained to the FBI director that the New York Police have not done a thorough job of investigating Jacobs's shooting. He feels that it might have been an attempted kidnapping. And that's where I come in. You know every attempted kidnapping threatening to cross state lines is a federal crime."

Drake burst into a laughter. "Didn't I tell you? You guys can make a federal case out of a clear blue sky. The fact of the matter is that you have come to provide a security blanket for Mr. Williams, so that his political contributions keep on flowing."

Reeves smiled; there was no point in arguing with that assumption. "Well, you can say that. It is a very sensitive matter. However, there are certain discrepancies, which I would like to discuss with you."

"Okay, go on," said Drake.

"I have read the files on Jacobs, Chimanski, and Judy Starsky. Jacobs, I cannot add anything. But the other two, they were shot by the same gun. I understand the gun was found in the trash compacter in Starsky's apartment. The autopsy shows there was powder around the wounds, but there were no powder burns. What do you make of that?"

"My first conclusion is that the medical examiner is crazy. Second conclusion is they might not have been shot from such a close range. That explains the powder and absence of burns."

Reeves sat back and shook his head from side to side, totally rejecting Drake's hypothesis. "FBI's ballistics experts have established that the gun was fired from within six inches. Another discrepancy. If Starsky killed the doctor in a fit of rage, why didn't he kill the wife at the same time? Why did he wait till evening to kill her?"

"You know he is a fag. Their behavior is most unpredictable."

"Is that your personal opinion or is there any scientific backing?" asked Reeves.

Drake said nothing.

Reeves continued, "I will let you in on a secret. I went over Dr. Chimanski's apartment. There were two unusual telephone calls. One was to a detective agency. He made the call at 5:00 P.M. the day before he was killed. He had an appointment with them at 4:00 P.M. the day he died. Second call was to Stoke-on-Trent, England, to a man called Dmitri Gustov. But the man had died two weeks earlier. Shot in the back of the head. Exact carbon copy of the murders of the two in your city."

Drake was looking straight ahead, partly stunned by the new information.

Reeves continued, "When you follow the chronological order, there is a definite sequence. Let's take the day before Chimanski was murdered. At 4:00 P.M., he makes a call to England. He discovers Gustov is dead. One hour later, he calls the detective agency, Three hours later, he was called to the hospital for an emergency. In the hospital he examined the patient and went straight to the operating room. One hour later he left the hospital, along with Nurse Starsky. The inevitable conclusion is the telephone call he made to the detective agency was his downfall. In other words, someone was bugging his telephone. As soon as someone knew he was going to a detective agency, they shut him up."

Drake lit a fresh cigarette. "I don't know. Your theory is farfetched. I think it is a simple case of passionate murder."

"And this powder business around the wound. This worries me too. Tests at the FBI lab show a gun silencer might have been used. Powder might have been implanted there to throw off the investigation."

"Hold your horses. Someone heard a shot in the corridor and called the police. So much for your silencer theory," said Drake.

"That might have been a diversion," insisted Reeves.

"Mr. FBI Agent, your problem is that you have got into your head that John Starsky is innocent. You are conforming whole evidence around that assumption."

"Wait a minute," said Reeves, "I am not saying John Starsky is innocent. As a matter of fact, I agree he should be your prime suspect. All I am saying is that these may not be simple jealousy murders. There may be organization behind them. That's why I would like to know where Mr. Starsky was on the 25th of February, the day Dmitri Gustov was murdered."

"I still say the moment Dr. Chimanski made a telephone call to the detective agency, he signed his own death certificate. So we go back to that event. I ask you for two favors. Number one, get hold of the telephone that was in Chimanski's apartment. The Bell Company has taken the telephone away. If you can find the phone, we can tear it apart and look for a bug inside. Number two, look for all new tenants within five hundred feet of Chimanski's apartment. I suppose any new tenant in the last three months. Five hundred feet is the maximum relaying distance for even the most sophisticated bugs."

Asked Drake, "His telephone might have been wiretapped?"

"That's not technically possible without the cooperation of the telephone company, or at least the cooperation of the apartment manager."

"I see. Something certainly is not kosher here."

"You are damn right," said Reeves.

"Do you think that the Chimanski and Starsky crowd were involved in some sort of drugs and somehow or other they got cold feet and the organization eliminated them?"

"Let's get out of this restaurant," said Reeves.

They walked down the Park Avenue. Reeves continued, "Certainly possible. But right now I will stick to your original theory that something is not kosher here."

"These damn immigrants. They are a double jeopardy to

this country. First they go on welfare. Second, they spy for countries of their origin," said Drake.

"Drake, tomorrow morning, I am flying to England. I want to have a gentleman's agreement with you. You stay off this investigation for two weeks. If I cannot prove a federal case by then, I will give you all the information I have collected. If I can, in that case, your problems are over anyway."

Reeves hailed a taxi and sped down Park Avenue.

Chapter 8

Reeves looked out of the cab. There were rows of houses lining each side of the road, red brick houses that had acquired a dull gray color from decades of coal dust deposited from industry and household fuel. On the tops of the houses, four chimneys were grouped together, some of them exuding thick smoke, which lingered over the houses on this drizzly day. The rows of houses were interrupted by frequent pubs and traffic lights. Outside the pubs at midday hung the thirsty customers. As the cab took a turn to the left, off Coronation Street, on James Street, the layout and the shapes of the houses had changed. There were twin houses now, joined together on one side, while on the other side there was a couple feet of space between them. There were a few yards of lawn in front of each house, interrupted by frequent rose bushes, which had not yet brought forth flower buds, but pale green petals were an assurance that they had survived the winter.

"Sir, here you are, 17 James Street," said the cab driver.

Reeves walked out of the cab and noticed the stink in the air. It was a definite reminder that the garbage strike was far from over. The government had not agreed to a 15 percent pay hike and a one-hour tea break. Reeves walked onto the short, narrow, cement walkway and rang the bell.

"Good morning, Mrs. Gustov. I am Jim Reeves."

"Come in, sir; a police officer called last night and said you would be coming."

Mrs. Gustov was a large woman. She had thick crude features. Her hair was coarse and light dark, mixed with streaks of gray. It was short and pressed against the scalp and upper part of her forehead. Her large dark eyes were a true reflection of her sensitiveness and revealed a soft heart linked to a will of steel. Two weeks earlier, when her husband died, she had secluded herself for a full week, along with her two sons, ten and twelve years old. When she emerged she had rearranged her priorities, charted her future, and with a renewed energy was ready to face the world again. Tragedy was no stranger to her. She had been on the roller coaster of life before. Prior to her coming to the Western world, she had lived in Moscow. Her husband had been a chemist in Moscow. Because of his political views, he had spent three years in Siberia. Those three years had changed her life. She had learned to live every day as it came. But that was a different tragedy. There was always that ray of hope. This time there was that awesome finality of death.

Jim Reeves sat in the chair in the small square living room, with the coal fire burning in the fireplace being the only source of heat.

"Mrs. Gustov, please accept my condolences on your husband's death." Reeves didn't know how best to respond to this ordinary, yet cultured woman.

"Officer, are you from New York?" she said.

"Yes, Ma'am. I am an FBI agent. I appreciate your seeing me at such a short notice."

"Would you like some tea?" asked Mrs. Gustov.

"No, thanks. I would like to get some information regarding your husband, if you don't mind."

"All right, Officer."

"Mrs. Gustov, have you any idea who could have killed your husband?" asked Reeves, while surveying the room.

"No, sir. I have absolutely no idea."

"Was anything stolen from your house?"

"Nothing was touched. His wallet was lying on the mantel of the fireplace. Not a single penny was missing."

Reeves looked at the mantel. There was a large portrait of the couple with their two sons.

Reeves smiled, "Ma'am, you have two handsome sons."

"Thank you, Officer. They are good boys."

"Had your husband any political affiliations?"

She looked at Reeves with her large dark eyes, not quite understanding what he meant.

"Ma'am, what I mean is, since he was an immigrant from Russia, did he belong to any societies or clubs that were against communism?"

"Yes, he did belong to a club called 'Survivor's Club.' He last went there two years ago. They generally discussed their horrifying experiences when they were prisoners in Siberia. This wasn't really a political club."

"Do you think he told you everything?" Every question he asked, he tried to put a little more pressure on her.

"Yes, sir, he did." Moisture had appeared in her eyes. "We are from the old country. We don't hide things. We are very close." She was talking about him as if he were still alive.

She couldn't contain her tears. They were streaming down her cheeks.

"He was a good husband. He was good to the boys. It is unbelievable that he survived three years in Siberia and was killed so senselessly in a safe place like England. They say no one carries guns here," she shook her head from side to side, "but I think things are changing here."

"Ma'am, did you emigrate here with the consent of the Russian authorities?"

"Yes, we did. First, we went to Israel, but he didn't like the constant talk of war there. So one year later, we came here. He hated violence."

"Did he communicate with any friends in Israel?" asked Reeves.

"No, sir," she said, wiping her eyes dry.

"Do you know Dr. Chimanski?"

"I never met him, but my husband talked a lot about him. Dr. Chimanski called here last week. He said he had written a letter to my husband."

Reeves, who up to now had been surveying the room while

asking questions, was now paying undivided attention to Mrs. Gustov.

"What did he say he wrote about?" he asked.

"I don't know. After I told him how Dmitri died, the whole conversation about the letter got lost."

"Did he say anything about the letter?"

"No, sir, he started talking about my husband. We never got back to the letter again."

"Where is this letter?"

"I looked for it. I cannot find it."

"Did he write to your husband regularly?" asked Reeves.

"No, sir, never before. This is the first time I heard of it."

"Did your husband say anything about this letter?"

"No, sir. Maybe you can ask Dr. Chimanski about the letter."

"Ma'am, Dr. Chimanski is dead. He was shot in the back of the head one week ago."

"God have mercy." She had slumped her face into her hands. "Who killed him?" Her face turned white as snow. Now she realized why the FBI man was taking unusual interest in her husband's death.

"We don't know. Can you remember anything else he said about the letter?"

"No, sir. He said he had written a letter to my husband and wanted to talk to him about the photograph he had sent. After I told him what had happened, we never got back to the letter again."

"What photograph?" Reeve's heart galloped a hundred miles per hour.

"I have no idea, Officer. I looked for the letter and the photograph. Cannot find either."

"Did he say whose photograph it was?"

"No, sir."

"Your husband called the post office three days prior to his death. He told them that he would be out of the city for three days and instructed them not to deliver mail for those days, for there had been some vandalism around. Why would he do that,

Mrs. Gustov?" Reeves thought the time was ripe to insinuate accusations.

"Sir, I don't understand why he did that, if it is true. He was home every day. In fact, they had been on strike for three weeks." Mrs. Gustov was looking into space. What does it matter how he died? She knew he was innocent. His life only revolved around his family and work. He never went anywhere alone. Now he had gone forever.

She tried to control her tears. She couldn't. She was sobbing.

Reeves got up from the chair and put his hand on her shoulder. How could he console a woman he had just met, particularly when he could not give her any information? He wasn't sure who was guilty and who was innocent. They were all playing their little games in this theatre of life, killing here and there and not leaving any clues behind.

"Officer, I know my husband was not a spy."

Reeves walked back to the chair, "Mrs. Gustov, I know what you are going through. But I would like you to understand that Dr. Chimanski's and your husband's deaths have some similarities. Both were Russian, both belonged to the same club; there were a letter and photograph, which we cannot trace. Both were murdered very similarly. The inevitable conclusion is that they both possessed some information that was so vital that the killer or killers executed these murders on both sides of the Atlantic. I would like you to concentrate on your husband's last few months. I mean, did he have any unusual calls or visitors, anything you noticed different about him, no matter how trivial it seems to you?"

"I cannot think of anything, Officer."

"I don't mean now. Try to relive your life in the last few months. If you turn up anything," he pulled a business card from his pocket and handed it to her, "anything trivial you find, please contact Officer Jones at Scotland Yard. He will know how to get in touch with me."

"Come to think—my husband did publish an article, 'Spring in Siberia,' in the local *Evening Times*. The editor was so impressed that he asked my husband to write more."

"Did he publish any more?"

"No, but he had been dictating his memoirs of when he was a prisoner in Siberia. The local press was going to serialize it."

"May I look at them?"

Mrs. Gustov fetched a brown bag from the next room. Reeves briefly looked at the papers and tapes. "Mrs. Gustov, it will take me a few hours to go through them. May I borrow them for a few days?"

She hesitated, "All right, but please don't lose them."

Stunned by the new information, she appeared perplexed. Had her husband been a spy all along? He couldn't be. But then the FBI man from New York could be right. Certainly there were a lot of similarities between the two murders. What did Dr. Chimanski want to talk to her husband about? What was this photograph all about? How could she be absolutely sure that her husband and Chimanski had not been communicating? Chimanski might have been calling him at his place of work. Perhaps that's why Chimanski called him at home, because he could not reach him at his place of work.

Reeves got up. "Mrs. Gustov, I appreciate your cooperation. If you turn up anything, please contact Inspector Jones. His telephone number is on the card."

"Good day, Officer," she said.

As Reeves walked out of the house on to the sidewalk, a blue car with white stripes pulled over. Reeves sat on the front seat. The man behind the wheel extended his hand.

"Inspector Jones, Harold Jones from Scotland Yard. I am the one you talked to on the phone this morning."

The inspector was perched comfortably behind the wheel, as if without the automobile his existence might have been a nightmare. He was a fat, short man in his late fifties. His face was furrowed and wrinkled. His scalp was shining. His forehead was a transition zone where a war was being waged between the natural processes of aging and his determination to stay young. Somewhere in that zone, there had been at one time, a distinct hairline.

"Nice to meet you in person, Inspector. I am Jim Reeves."

"I hope you enjoy your stay here." Jones had abruptly withdrawn his hand and was fondling the wheel as he drove away.

"I'm afraid that's not possible. I am taking a flight to Zurich at 4:00 P.M."

"I thought you were going to stay here for a couple of days?"

"I know. Something has come up since I talked with you this morning."

"Mr. Reeves, what do you say?"

"I don't know. All I know is that people are being murdered on both continents. No definite motives. Everyone seems to be as innocent as Snow White, but I know among these Snow Whites, somewhere there is a Wicked Witch."

"What do you think about her?" asked Jones.

"Oh. I don't know. It's hard to say."

Jones nodded. "So your sudden departure to Zurich this afternoon, what does that mean?"

"I think we might have a fresh lead. There is this private detective. He thinks he has important information."

"This letter. What is it all about?" inquired Inspector Jones.

"I have absolutely no idea. She says she cannot find the letter. We know the source. It was written by Chimanski. I have no idea what it could possibly contain."

"I say, this bloke Chimanski was a Russian Jew, wasn't he?"

"Yes, he was."

"Well. So was Gustov. They belong to the same 'Survivor's Club.' I cannot speak for New York, but London has a lot of militants. Maybe they were both spying for Israel and the Arabs got wind of it."

"Okay, that makes sense to a certain degree, but two events in this death saga fall out. Number one, the sequence of events is all reversed. If the killers knew that the letter had been written by Chimanski and mailed, they would have killed Chimanski and then gone after the letter and then gotten rid of Gustov. The second fallout, the day before Chimanski was murdered, he contacted a private detective agency in New York. That doesn't make sense either. Imagine a spy getting help from the Yellow

Pages. That damn letter is the key to all this death drama."

The car was out of the congested streets of Stoke-on-Trent, now speeding on the motorway toward the airport.

"I have the feeling that you haven't spilled all your guts out, as you Americans say," said Jones firmly.

Reeves was taken back by Jones's abruptness. He had reckoned him to be a typically mild British officer.

"Well, we obviously have a new lead, but this might take us nowhere."

"That's interesting." Jones voice had become completely monotonous. "We have one lead too, but as you say, it might not lead us anywhere."

Reeves, who up until now was scanning the English countryside, suddenly put his hand on the dashboard and turned toward Jones.

"Jones, don't play these little games with me. Three murders have been committed, and you are trying to hold back information."

"Mr. Reeves, that's interesting, sir. You think you are entitled to information I dig up, yet you are not willing to share the information you have in your possession."

"Haven't I got clearance from Scotland Yard? Tell me. Haven't I?" Reeves was furious.

"I know you have, but doesn't it make sense that if we have to work together, we must share the information?"

"I understand. You know how it works. Your bosses must get their clearance for you from the FBI and CIA; otherwise, I will be hanging from the lamp post outside the Pentagon." To calm his nerves, Reeves took out his pipe from his pocket and proceeded to pack it with tobacco, with the devotion of a priest paying his homage to the Buddha. He had made sure the tobacco was packed to perfect compactness. There was no point in further arguing with Jones. Given the jealousy between FBI and Scotland Yard, this man Jones was going to need a lot of arm-twisting before he cooperated.

"Well, chap." Jones had suddenly mellowed. "I'll put all my cards on the table, and you pick up the ones you want. Let's go back to the Gustovs. I made some inquiries in the neighborhood. Two ten-year-old lads were playing some car games. Guess what one car number appeared three days prior to Dmitri Gustov's death? The car is registered in London, belongs to a car rental agency, the Economy Car Rentals. It was rented to a man called David Brown. The rest you have guessed already. David Brown and the address he gave are both fictitious."

Reeves, who up until now had stayed reasonably calm, suddenly exploded. "You think that's funny, don't you?"

"I don't understand what you mean," said Jones.

"You think that's funny. I have flown all the way from New York to interview this woman and you purposely withheld this information. Don't you realize that if I had this information, I could have squeezed her for a little bit more."

"Old chap, on the other hand, look at the other side of the coin. We don't want to scare her. We don't want to give her the feeling that she is involved. Right now I have more detectives following her than the Queen of England."

To Reeves, this sort of reasoning was superfluous. Jones had insulted him as if he didn't know how to question a suspect. "Inspector Jones, let me show you the other side of the coin. If you were in New York, I would have thrown you out of the car."

Jones smiled. Reeves thought that compounded his original crime of arrogance.

Jones continued, "So David Brown does not exist. More disturbing is the fact that the photocopy of the license shows the forgery of the driver's license was a perfect job, complete in every detail."

Reeves had returned to the world of logic. "That means there is a big organization behind these murders."

"Precisely, old chap. Someone does not want to leave any clues behind."

Jones parked the car in the two-way zone in front of the departures entrance to the airport.

"Okay, Jones. My flight is due in forty minutes. Why don't you go ahead." Reeves thought Jones's cooperation had been less than satisfactory. But nevertheless, the information regarding the car was significant. It confirmed his own suspicions that there was more to it than met the eye.

Jones, somehow, was able to drag his fat body from behind the wheel. "Old chap, before you go, let me give you a peace offering in the temple of arguments and compromises, the English pub."

Before Reeves could say anything, Jones dragged him toward the pub.

As Jones gulped and Reeves sipped the warm English beer, Reeves realized he was partially wrong. After all, Jones was not such a bad guy. Jones had his American counterpart stay in England at least for a few days. He was repeatedly talking about how great the city of London was, how pretty the English countryside was, but then there was his favorite place, the English pub. "When all is said and done," he told Reeves, "the English pub is one hell of an institution." He had lamented that with the immigrants, the English scene was changing, "England will never be the same again." Suddenly his eyes were filled with contempt.

All 250 pounds of him packed into the wooden chair, after gulping down the whole pint of beer, was trying to maneuver out of the chair to lay his hands on another pint.

"None for me," Reeves told him.

Jones looked at the half-finished beer in front of Reeves, "Old chap, I should have guessed. You Americans like fancy cocktails, but I can assure you that the bloke behind the bar doesn't know how to mix them."

Reeves got up. "I think I better check in." As both walked toward the Swiss Air counter, Reeves took his pipe out and lit it.

"Jones, you are okay. I think we can work together. Let me brief you on my trip to Zurich. There is this guy, Stewart, who works for a private detective agency. He is in Zurich protecting a businessman. He has accidentally stumbled onto some important information. Well, as a matter of fact, he thinks we should looked into a safety deposit box in the National Bank in Zurich. The United States Government has not been able to persuade the bank authorities to open the box. The president of the bank has

said that the only way we can look into the box is to break into
the bank and we have accepted that challenge."

Jones looked at him with a combination of disbelief and
amazement.

Reeves had disappeared into the departure lounge.

"Cheerio . . . old chap . . . good luck!"

CHAPTER 9

ZURICH

Had face been a dictate of his profession, Albert Stewart would have been a business executive. He had a square face with a large forehead claiming a major impact on his features. His sideburns were high, with not a hair out of place. His hair was brushed straight back, with two bald patches on each side escorting a tuft of hair left in the middle, an appearance that was meant to raise a man from his grave and sell him a junk Toyota. There were two up and down permanent furrows on his forehead, which only told a partial story of a man who had chosen and cherished a dangerous life. Three years ago, he had been fired from the FBI. His boss, Jim Reeves, at that time had conceded that Stewart was a fearless and conniving man, but that was not enough. A different wind was blowing in those days. Bloodletting was needed to get rid of poison from the FBI. Jim Reeves, his immediate boss, had spotted the prominent jugular vein and aimed right at it. Stewart's career was over. If he had his own choice, he would have let Stewart go with a warning, but his shoulder was merely a resting place for the rifle. Somebody higher up was pulling the trigger.

As an FBI agent, Stewart had done several unauthorized break-ins and phone tappings and worse than that, he had refused to admit that something wrong had been done. "What good is the secret agent, if he doesn't have a free hand?" The more he defended, the more he was branded defiant. For Stewart, this was a calamity. The only world he knew, of intrigues and improvisations, had been suddenly snatched away from him. As reality dumped its full load on him, he realized it was not only the livelihood that he had lost, it was as if an important part of him had been mutilated, amputated, and thrown away.

Stewart heard a knock at the door of his hotel room. He opened the door. "I'll be damned, if it's not the famous Jim Reeves, the leader of the firing squad." He shook Reeves's hand violently and pulled him into the room.

Jim Reeves wasn't surprised. He knew his reception was going to be less than optimal.

"You still don't believe me, do you? I was just carrying out the orders of my superiors," said Reeves.

The furrows on Stewart's forehead reached a ferocious depth. "Let's not talk about the past. Pour yourself a drink and talk about the future."

Reeves poured himself a Scotch and watched Stewart gulp down his favorite drink, rum and Sea Cola.

Reeves persisted, "But I want to clear the air before I go any further."

"Let's get out of this damn shit. I don't want to see any artificial tears. Let's get down to business." Stewart's eyes were still fixed on Reeves.

"Al, give me a break, will you?" pleaded Reeves.

"Sure, sure . . . I will give you a break. Did you give me a break? Do you know what happened to me after I was fired? My wife left me. My friends deserted me. I ended up in a mental asylum. One damn stroke of your pen and my whole life crumbled right in front of my eyes." He had lowered his voice to a whisper. He was staring into space.

There was chilling silence in the room. Reeves didn't know how to break that silence. He wasn't quite sure how to restart the conversation without touching off another apopletic rage.

"Now you are asking for a break," Stewart broke the silence.

Reeves realize his mild manner wasn't taking him anywhere. "Can't you get it through your head that I don't make the rules for the FBI? I was merely following the orders of my superiors. Those fat cats in the Congress, they make the rules."

"But don't you see the point," insisted Stewart. "How can you collect information, if you don't bend the rules?"

"I know. I know. But you were actually breaking the law."

"Okay." Stewart walked to the makeshift bar in his room and poured rum and cola into the glass simultaneously. "Okay, you play the game according to the rules. If you have your act together, why are you sniffing around me like a starving dog?"

"Al, you haven't changed, have you? You are the same old stubborn bastard." Reeves tried to change his strategy.

Stewart smiled a little. He wasn't going to give up. "You have drawn a blank card, haven't you? That's why you are here."

"Well," Jim was trying to dodge the question.

"By the way, have you seen those shows put up by blubbers in Florida?" said Stewart.

Reeves looked at Stewart, half amazed.

"You know those slimy animals, dolphins and whales, which will jump fifty feet in the air and then dash to their trainer for a handful of fish," Stewart smiled.

"Yes, I have seen those shows. What about them?"

"Well, your FBI works the same way. Your bosses tell you when to sit and when to shoot. So long as you understand the signals and don't use your brain, you are okay and get promotions. When you use your brain, you can open your mouth as wide as a hippopotamus does, but you won't get the stinking fish."

Reeves felt a little hurt, his pride wounded. "I am sure somewhere in there is a punch line and possibly a message."

"Yes, you are damn right there is one. The Russians know the name of the game. They may not know how to control dolphins, but they certainly know how to control the FBI and the CIA. While you people are playing the game according to the rules made by slobs in the Congress, the Russians are changing the rules all the time. Tell me, confess, you don't have a stinking clue, do you?"

"Well, we are following some leads," said Reeves.

"Well, let's see where you stand. Dr. Chimanski is dead. His nurse friend, what's her name, she is gone. The Sea Cola tycoon, he almost died. They all knew each other and you cannot connect them."

Jim Reeves, who up to now was trying to make small talk, was suddenly perplexed. This was the information he was going to feed to Stewart to win his confidence.

"How the hell do you know all this?" asked Reeves.

"Well, I have my sources . . . *The New York Times*," smiled Stewart.

"In that case, you better expand your sources. Start reading *The Times* of London. Two weeks ago another friend of Chimanski was shot dead in Stoke-on-Trent, England. A carbon copy murder of Chimanski."

"Who is this guy?" asked Stewart.

"Dmitri Gustov," continued Reeves, "Anyway, if you follow the theory of the common denominator, Chimanski is the central point. Everything he touches turns to ashes."

"Interesting theory," nodded Stewart, "But like any other theory, it has to be proven or rejected. See my point? If you were a free agent, by now you would be far ahead. Look at me. In three days I have collected more information than you have in three months."

"But you struck oil," said Reeves.

"What the hell is that supposed to mean? I broke into his hotel room, planted miniature amplifiers under his coat lapels, and bugged his telephone. That's not being lucky. That's planning. Do you realize the information I have collected is through illegal means?"

Reeves put his glass on the table. "Makes no difference. You are a private citizen now. Besides, you are not in U.S. territory."

Stewart burst into laughter. "So you and the FBI endorse my illegal activities in a foreign country."

"So . . . what do you think he is up to?" asked Reeves.

His manner was subdued now. "I don't know what he is up to, but I know what you should be up to. You should look into the Safety Box Number 38 in the National Bank."

"I know we tried to convince the Swiss Government to open the safety box. I am afraid that's out of the question."

"So we are in a blind alley. Where do we go from here?" asked Stewart.

"You are damn right. We are in a blind alley. We have no

option but to break into that bank," replied Reeves.

Stewart burst into laughter. "Jim, you know what your problem is? You are watching too much of 'Charlie's Angels.'"

Reeves didn't think that was funny. "But we are going to break into that bank."

Stewart still thought Reeves's idea was ridiculous. "And how do you propose to do that?"

"Well, as a matter of fact, we were hoping that you would do it for us."

"What the hell is that supposed to mean?" Stewart squished his cigarette into the depths of the ashtray and dashed to the bar for a refill of his favorite drink.

"The FBI cannot break the rules, but as a private citizen you can," explained Reeves.

"Oh, no. I am not going into that bank. Too risky. They have alarms everywhere. They don't even have the death penalty. I will be stuck in the hole for twenty years."

"Al, relax, will you? Every detail has been worked out."

"You smart ass, I bet you have. Give me a battalion of marines, and I will open every box for your inspection."

Reeves smiled, pursed his lips and shook his head from side to side, "No, sir. Guns have no place in such a sensitive mission. Not so late in the twentieth century anyway. We will break into the bank with space technology."

"I understand," Stewart smiled. "So you expect me to land into the bank from a satellite."

Reeves smiled, "Stewart, will you stop fooling around? Try and concentrate on what I am saying."

There was a knock at the door.

"That must be David Moore," said Reeves.

"Who the hell is he?" asked Stewart.

"He is CIA's Radio Shack."

Stewart dashed toward the door, "Tell me, am I expecting any more guests?"

"Who knows? But if there are any more, they are going to be gate-crashers," said Reeves.

David Moore was a tall, skinny man, who looked like a

scarecrow dressed with reject clothes from the Salvation Army. His thin, crudely trimmed mustache merged imperceptibly into his partially shaven face. His crooked, worn-out brown tie was a perfect complement to the rest of his clothes.

"Come in, Dave, meet Albert Stewart. Al used to work for the FBI," said Reeves.

"Mr. Moore, can I get you a drink?" asked Stewart.

"No sir, I don't drink." He put his small suitcase by his side. "I had a cup of tea before I came."

Reeves lit his pipe. "Al, if you ever decide to break into Fort Knox, the man to get in touch with would be David Moore. David either has or will invent a gadget for you."

Stewart found that amusing, although David Moore was a little embarrassed. He felt uneasy in the present company, for his life was built around technology, not around contrivances. True, he had met the smartest spies, but he had never let their life-style influence him. He was an inventor of a different kind. He was the chief technician at the CIA.

Reeves continued, "Gentlemen, it is time we got down to business in detail. Al, we will give you complete details of the mission. After that, you can make up your mind whether you want to participate or not." Reeves walked to the bar and poured himself another drink. "The purpose of our mission is to retrieve the Safety Box Number 38 from the National Bank in Zurich. This has to be done without coercing or confronting any individual. When all of this comes out, who knows when, you will realize that you have participated in the most important spy drama of the century. Al, if you decide to undertake this mission, you will enter the bank at 1:00 P.M. tomorrow. It is full of customers at that time. Lunch-time customers, the busiest time for the banks. No guns, please. We have rented Safety Box Number 28, which is by the side of Safety Box Number 38."

Moore opened his suitcase and pulled out a steel box from inside. "This is an exact replica of the box we have rented for you. In this box is a half million-dollar technology."

Stewart was surprised. To him it looked like cheap Japanese transistor radio.

Reeves continued, "So you enter the bank at 1:00 P.M. Go to the bank teller and ask for Number 3171943. The safety boxes, as you know, are in the basement. Take the box with you in a small suitcase. So you switch the boxes in the bank. I mean, take the box out from Number 28 and replace it with the box that David has brought for you."

Reeves looked at Moore. "Dave, do you want to pick up from there?"

Moore opened the box again. "Well, as I said, this box has a very sophisticated technology built inside. At 9:00 P.M. the computer inside the box will activate a laser beam. This laser beam has a precise cutting ability of two centimeters, which is exactly the thickness of the partitions between the boxes in the bank. The beam will travel in a rectangular manner and cut along the edge of the partition."

Stewart was sitting there stunned, absolutely amazed how technology had been harnessed to rob a bank. Now he knew what Reeves meant when he said he was going to break into the bank with space technology. He asked, "How about the heat generated by this activity?"

Moore replied, "You are right. That could be a problem. That is why we are taking six hours so that there is enough time for the heat to dissipate. Otherwise the laser beam could easily finish the job in one minute."

Said Stewart, "So next day I retrieve the box through the fallen partition?"

"Exactly," answered Reeves.

Moore interjected, "Not quite. Second day you switch off the computer. Otherwise, that evening another partition will fall. You see this green button? Push it and a green light will appear, which means the computer is inactivated."

"And what about the smoke generated by the laser beam? You know they have smoke alarms everywhere."

Moore replied, "That is no problem. We do not expect any smoke. But in case there is any, we have in-built absorbent chemicals in the box. I don't want to bore you with the chemical details."

Stewart thought he might as well ask this, "Is it radioactive?" Not that it would have made any difference to him.

"Some parts are, but they are all well insulated."

Stewart was looking straight ahead at Moore. "How long do we keep the box I retrieve?"

Moore said, "No idea. That's not my game."

Reeves picked up the question, "Depends upon what we find."

"What do you expect?"

"I don't know. My hunch is that it is going to be fascinating."

The three of them were like children hanging around the tree on Christmas Eve, playing guessing games with their presents.

"What do I get out of this?" asked Stewart.

Reeves walked to the window. From the twentieth floor, the automobiles on the street looked like large match boxes on wheels. "Ten thousand dollars. I speak for both the FBI and the CIA. I don't need to tell you that these two agencies are the only set-ups in our democratic society where deceit, flat lies, and denials are a way of life. You are not going to be made an exception. If you are caught, the Secretary of State will disown you, but that does not mean that we shall forget you and to that end, I offer you my word."

For a while, there was absolute silence in the room. Then Reeves looked at Stewart, "What do you say?"

Stewart smiled, "Well, I guess I have a date with the computer tomorrow at one o'clock."

CHAPTER 10

At the peak of the lunch hour, Stewart walked out of the National Bank. If yesterday's work was kindergarten stuff, today's was no more difficult than the first grade. Why the hell the CIA and FBI were paying him ten thousand dollars to do this kid stuff, he could not figure out. Maybe the agencies want to keep their hands clean so that ten years from now when dirty linen is washed in the Congress, no bloodstains would be found on their hands. They were getting smart. They had been burnt before. Maybe the FBI realizes that it made a blunder when they fired him three years ago and now want to cleanse their conscience with the holy water of dollars.

Yesterday all he had to do was to place the box containing the computer in Compartment 28 of the safety vault. Today at lunch time, when he went back there, everything had been as described by Moore. He opened the door of the Safety Box 28 and pulled the box out. The partition between the Compartments 28 and 38 was still there. He took a small magnet from his pocket, stuck it to the partition, and pulled the partition out. The laser beam had made a clean cut along the edge of the plate. Through the fallen partition, he pulled the box from Number 38 into Compartment 28, retrieved it, and placed it in his small suitcase. There was a burglar camera, which he thought was off. Anyway, to be extra cautious, he positioned himself between the camera and his maneuvers. He didn't know why he was taking all these precautions. The bank teller had left him for a while. As far as she was concerned, she couldn't care if he stored a neutron bomb there.

As he walked along the sidewalk, he knew that two-thirds of his mission was over, the remaining one-third would be completed when he returned the box to the bank. If everything went smoothly, and there was no reason why not, Reeves was sure to recommend him back into the FBI. In spite of his misgivings, the FBI was his shining star. The small suitcase felt like a ton of weight. He walked over to the rented car, which he had parked a block away from the bank. He put the suitcase on the front seat. As he drove away, the snow appeared as cotton floccules dancing in front of the windshield. As the car picked up speed, they were now tiny missiles traveling at a terrific speed. As they hit the windshield, their energy dissipated instantaneously.

What the hell did the box contain? Espionage papers? But the box was too heavy. Could it be precious stones, but again the box was too heavy. Gold? Good possibility, except that the man was a millionaire. He wouldn't be interested in storing a few ounces of gold, probably peanuts for him. And besides, the CIA wouldn't be interested in going through all this trouble to look at a few blocks of solid gold.

His curiosity by now was overwhelming. He opened the suitcase and then he opened the safety box. He knew the place must be swarming with CIA agents. He kept his eyes on the road. With his right hand, he felt the inside of the box. There were a number of small bottles packed haphazardly, with pieces of foam packing in between. As he waited at the traffic light, he took one bottle out and looked at it through the corner of his eye. They were six-ounce miniature Sea Cola bottles, gold color with bold black imprint, "Golden Anniversary Sea Cola Celebration Size. The Best Thing." He put his hand in the box and felt around. It was full of same size bottles. What the hell was that suppose to mean? That was somewhat of a let-down for him. He had expected something more exciting, like precious stones or classified documents. Not only that, the whole mission was so dull. Although the mission was supposed to be important, its actual mechanics were bland. No real danger to himself. There were no intrigues. There were no imaginary pitfalls. There was nothing left to chance. But what the hell did he care? He was being paid ten thousand dollars by the agency.

Stewart took the box to his room. Moore and Reeves were waiting for him.

Said Reeves, "Any problems?"

"No," replied Stewart.

Reeves looked at Moore. "Dave, you handle it from now onward."

Moore put a pair of surgical gloves on and fingerprinted the inside of the box. Gently he lifted a bottle out of the box and looked at it carefully. Stewart walked over to look at the inside of the box as if this was the first time he was looking at its contents. He asked Reeves, "What do you make of these bottles?"

"Right now I have no idea. But soon we will have an answer. In the meantime, I want to thank you on behalf of the United States Government. Soon we will have an orchestra going to welcome you back into the FBI."

Stewart simply looked ahead, his eyes slightly moist with emotion. "Jim, isn't it strange? Four years ago I was busting my chops for the FBI, and they fired me. Now, I accidentally stumble onto some information, and they claim me a messiah, wanting me to come back to the promised land."

Replied Reeves, "Sure. Don't you kow all adventures in life are a matter of timing, and talking of timing, I will see you at nine sharp tomorrow morning." Reeves and Moore walked out of the room, along with the box.

Stewart slumped into the chair. Sure, promised land he was getting back into, the only life he knew, of intrigues, instantaneous decisions, times of exhilaration moments after escaping from danger. There was no parallel to that sort of life. He knew as soon as his role was over, Reeves was sure to recommend him back into the FBI. Soon, he would be getting out of his monotonous detective work, which consisted of either protecting rich people from imaginary enemies or sitting in his car on Manhattan streets on cold, wintry nights, collecting evidence of adulteries so that wives and husbands could tear each other apart. This wasn't his cup of tea. This was substitute living.

This was Stewart's first trip to Zurich. He was very excited about the adventure he had undertaken today. He poured himself a drink, his favorite drink, rum and cola. He walked to the window and looked out. The temperature outside had dropped considerably in the last two hours. The earlier snow had changed into tiny iceballs, which, as they hit the glass window, made a tinkling sound. Some of them were sticking to the outside of the glass. As he kept watching them, the inside of the glass was getting foggier from his breath and the tiny iceballs now had yellow and green halos around them. As it got still foggier, the balls got more distorted and the colors faded away. Stewart thought, at times like these, one needs a friend who is real close to you and can admire your work. A friend who can look into your eyes and state in pure innocence, "Congratulations, you have done an excellent job." He wished his wife was there. She loved and admired this sort of work. He lay down on the bed. He was exhausted. Due to the excitement, he had not slept a wink last night. Suddenly the world had taken a new meaning for him. He was back in the mainstream of the style of life he loved so much.

It was 6:00 P.M. now. The snow had stopped. The streets were full of people going in all directions. A few tourists were whiling away their time looking at display windows. He walked toward the left on the sidewalk. As dark thickened and the street lights reflected off the fresh snow on the pavement, everything around looked neat and white. Somewhere along the pavement, a plump lady with a large moon face was rocking a small tin box. An occasional passerby would drop a coin in there and as the coin dropped in the box, simultaneously she would utter a word, which Stewart didn't understand. It must be "thank you" in German. As he reached the crossroad, he felt a burst of cold wind hitting his face, for here he had lost the protection of the tall buildings. He crossed the road and went into the bar around the corner. He sat on the stool on the counter. The bar was deserted at this time. He ordered his favorite drink.

"Are you American?" He heard a soft voice.

He looked to the left side. There was a girl in her twenties sitting on a nearby table. "Yes, Ma'am." Stewart looked at little startled.

"I knew it. Americans always order 'on the rocks.' Others 'on the ice.' " She smiled a little. That was obviously not her natural smile. There was little quiver on her lips. Stewart looked at her attentively.

"May I join you?" he said.

"Sure, come along here."

Stewart walked over to the table, "I am Albert Stewart."

"Olivia Duesler," she said.

"I like the combination, Swedish accent with an excellent command of English."

"Simple explanation. I was in New York for two years," said Olivia.

"Did you like New York?"

"The city itself was very cruel, but I met a lot of interesting people there. Are you here on business?" she asked.

"Yes, I work for IBM. Were you a student in New York?"

"No, I was secretary in a small firm, but soon I found the work boring and I switched to an escort service."

Stewart, who up to now had been sipping his drink, suddenly gulped down a mouthful. He tried to avoid asking the next logical question, but his curiosity and strange pathological excitement overpowered him. "Did you find that exciting?"

"Initially, it was exciting, but later on it became like any other job."

"What do you do here?"

"Same service."

Stewart looked at her. She was looking straight ahead at the bar. Her lips were tightly held with a slight tremor of her cheek muscles, her eyes narrowed, reflecting a contempt for the man-dominated society, as if Stewart had been selected to represent that society. Stewart knew the last two questions stood *prima facie* evidence against man's callousness and indifference to a just society. As those thoughts were crossing his mind, she looked at him with a smile and her eyes reflecting the curiosity of a child who has discovered a seashell on the beach.

"Would you like another drink?" asked Stewart.

"Why not?"

The guilt feelings that were clouding his mind had disappeared, and now he felt a surge of warmth. At least she had been incredibly honest. He wasn't a veteran at visiting houses of ill repute, but he had an idea that's not the way they generally operate.

"Would you care to join me for a bite? I am famished," said Stewart.

"All right."

As Stewart helped her with the coat, he took a deep breath to get the full impact of the sensuous cologne she was wearing. He had not been out with a woman for a year. This wasn't normal but then he wasn't living in a normal environment. His thoughts wandered back to her again. How incredibly honest she was.

Stewart was tossing about in his bed. He looked at his watch. It was 6:00 A.M. He tried to sleep, but as he closed his eyes, a sickening ache started in his legs. As this intensified, he felt a sudden surge of intense heat rushing toward his feet. The sickening ache kept building into a tempo, and the heat kept building into a furnace until they merged into each other. The rest of his body felt ice cold. He curled up as a natural defense against this strange phenomenon. The sunlight was entering through a small slit between the partially closed halves of the curtain. He tried to concentrate on the light, but his eyes were getting heavier and everything was falling out of focus. The sunlight now had colorful wavy lines on either side. His whole body was aching now. He lay there with his jaw listless, drooping with a wide gap between his jaws through which he was breathing shallowly with a tremendous effort.

He tried to close his eyes. A sudden feeling of nausea came over him. As if to reassure himself, he immediately opened his eyes. He had no doubt that all this was a big hangover from the variety of drinks he had last night. He had another shivering. His entire body was shaking as if rocked by a powerful earthquake. His mouth was the bark of a seasoned wood. He gulped down the Sea Cola from the half-finished bottle. The shivering passed over. Drenched with cold sweat, he lay there exhausted, partly relieved that the horrible nightmare was over. He closed his eyes. He felt relaxed.

The last thing he remembered was the girl mixing a drink for him. He tried to remember what happened afterwards, but there was a complete lapse. Her appearance still lingered in his mind. In no time the girl had disappeared, replaced by a large ant, which was climbing up a huge mountain. The ant was about half the size of the mountain. It kept inching towards the top, Stewart opened his eyes. The ant was gone. He closed his eyes again. The ant was back again. It had climbed almost to the top and was looking straight at him. Its eyes were spherical, bulging, bloody, and they reflected awful concentration and frigidity. He was there helplessly waiting for the inevitable to happen. The huge ant slipped down to the bottom of the mountain. As if unperturbed by all this, it started its journey up again. He was terrified.

He suddenly woke up. His heart was beating at a terrific speed. He turned to the left to look at the clock. He felt an intense headache shooting down the back of his neck. His aches, fever, and shivering had all merged into a complex feeling of listlessness and extreme lethargy. He knew he was running a high fever. Probably flu. Plenty of it in New York when he left there. He put the light on. The light was so intense that he turned his head to the other side, and as he did so the intense headache shooting down the neck hit him like lightning. With considerable effort he sat on the side of the bed. His headache was getting unbearable. He sat there supporting his head with both hands as if it was going to fall off his neck. Then he stood up to test his faculties. He picked up the phone and saw every article in the room going around and around. First this was slow and sequential, but soon the rotation picked up a terrific speed. Everything around him was going around in one direction, and he was rotating in the opposite direction. The articles in the room started to appear fuzzy. The telephone dropped out of his hand. The next moment he fell to the floor. He hit his head against the nightstand. He lay there motionless. He felt nothing. He was in a coma.

Reeves had been trying to reach him since nine o'clock. There was a constant busy signal from his room. The telephone operator had confirmed that the telephone was off the hook. With a duplicate key, the manager and Reeves entered the room. Stewart was still lying at the same place where he fell. Bleeding from the gash in the head had stopped. The nearby carpet was soaked with blood. Reeves felt his carotids. They were full and bouncing. Then he touched his forehead. It was on fire with fever. His face was covered with sweat beads, like early morning spring dew sticks to the tender leaves of the catalpa tree. Stewart was in a deep coma.

Reeves stood up and looked all around. "What the hell happened?" The manager called the ambulance without answering. Reeves sat on the chair trying to make sense out of all this. Too many things had happened too quickly.

CHAPTER 11

By 1:00 P.M., after running a whole battery of tests, the doctors had reached a working diagnosis. They had taken syringefuls of blood. They had inserted tubes everywhere. They had stuck a needle into his spine, to look at fluid of his brain. Reeves walked into the emergency room as Stewart was being wheeled toward the intensive-care unit. A tall, blonde, Swedish doctor had gotten hold of Reeves, thoroughly convinced that Reeves was going to provide the missing link.

The doctor extended his hand out, "I am Dr. Shoemaker."

"Jim Reeves." He shook the doctor's hand.

"How is he, Doctor?" asked Reeves.

"His condition is unchanged. Let's go to the next room, my office. I would like to get some history from you."

"Are you staying together?" asked the doctor. He had a strong accent. Reeves had to strain his ears to understand him.

"Yes, we are staying in the same hotel."

"Your friend, still in coma. Very high fever, 104°. All the tests, up to now, show he has viral infection of the brain, viral encephalitis."

"How did he get that so fast, Doctor? I was with him at lunchtime yesterday; he was fine," said Reeves.

"Did he complain of a headache?" The doctor ran his fingers through his hair.

"If he had any, he didn't mention it to me."

"Did he look sick?" persisted the doctor.

"No, Doctor, he looked fine."

"What is his job?"

"He works for IBM, computer engineer."

"Does he handle any chemicals?" The doctor was taking brief notes at the same time.

"No. It is a desk job." Reeves could not tell him his real job.

The doctor sat in his swivel chair, his head resting against the wall, his hands folded in his lap. "Mr. Reebes," he was pronouncing "V" as "b," "We are running more tests on your friend. It seems he has a flu-like infection of his brain. This can be serious."

"How serious, Doctor?" asked Reeves.

"Can be fatal. There is a flu going around in New York; I think he picked up the infection there," continued the doctor. "Some people are tough. They just won't complain unless they are really down."

"Yes, Doc. Tough bird he is. Sometimes too tough. Do you think he will make it?" Reeves needed a definite answer from the doctor, for he had a million things to take care of.

"I don't know. It is difficult to say. If he pulls through the next twenty-four hours, his chances will improve."

"Doctor, could he have been poisoned?"

The doctor pondered the question for a while. He puckered his lips and looked straight ahead. "Do you mean food poisoning? It doesn't look like. No, I don't think so. His clinical picture and tests all point toward a severe viral infection."

"Is it contagious?" asked Reeves.

"Not likely. It's like an ordinary flu. In some people, like Mr. Stewart, it would hit the brain. There is no way to predict or prevent this complication. What is puzzling is that it hit him so fast, but I believe he was sick for a while and wasn't complaining."

Reeves hesitated a little. "I respect your judgment, Doctor. But do you think you could ask for a brain specialist to look at him?"

Dr. Shoemaker showed no resentment. "I have already requested a consultation from Dr. Bohnmeir. He is a neurologist."

Dr. Shoemaker got up from his chair. "Mr. Reeves, I will get back to you if anything new develops. Leave your telephone number where you can be reached."

Next morning at 6:00 A.M., Reeves got a call from the hospital. The doctor would like to see him immediately. Reeves looked out from the hotel room window on the twentieth floor. The sun had just appeared on the horizon. One minute there was darkness, the very next minute light was erupting from all directions. Tall buildings were emerging like slowly arousing giants, testimony to the fact that the man has to do what he has to do, irrespective of who gets destroyed in the process.

Stewart had died one hour earlier. His temperature had kept soaring up, in spite of all treatments prescribed by the doctors. His coma was relentless. Finally his heart started galloping away at a very fast rate with no rhythm or rhyme. The doctors gave him electric shocks, but his heart kept slipping into that fast beat. Then the heart stopped. As a last effort, they injected medications into the heart to restart it, but there was no response. Then they gave up. Stewart lay there with his eyes open, a plastic tube coming out of his mouth. The intravenous fluid was still pouring into his right arm. He had multiple bruises and needle marks on both arms, where unsuccessful attempts were made to start intravenous injections. The doctor put on his white coat and walked out of the room. The job of converting the corpse into respectable form was left to the nurses, who, like well-trained professionals, went over the body, disconnecting various contraptions, pulling out IV's and various tubes. Finally, they pulled down his eyelids over the eyeballs and put a white sheet over his head.

"Mr. Reeves, I am sorry. There was nothing else we could do. He died one hour ago," said Dr. Shoemaker.

"Thanks, Doctor. I realize you did everything."

"He had an overwhelming infection. Who is his closest relative?"

"No one. He was divorced."

"I am afraid I will have to insist on an autopsy. According to Swiss law, this becomes a coroner's case. The coroner will arrange the autopsy."

"Could this be done in America? I can arrange special transport."

"I am sorry. In this sort of situation, we have to establish the diagnosis," persisted the doctor.

"But Doctor, I thought you already knew the diagnosis." Reeves had hoped the doctor would change his mind.

"I know it is a virus, but we have to identify the exact virus. Besides, there are public health problems."

One hour later Reeves walked out of the hospital. It was a clear chilly day, with a slow wind blowing from the west. He crossed the road and looked into the river. It was a sheet of ice. Through an occasional crack, he saw the water underneath. Slanting rays of the sun reflected an array of colors. He looked at them more attentively. Apart from violet and deep orange, he could not pick up any other colors, although he distinctly knew they were there in nature's magnificent display.

Up the street, across the bridge, the shop window displayed glittering Swiss watches. There was such a contrast between the man's display in the windows and nature's display all around. Who knows who is right and who is wrong, but certainly man was on a collision course with nature. Everything man did in the name of humanity and justice. He killed, he murdered, he subjugated and he humiliated in the name of humanity.

He was getting aware of the chill all around. He took the pipe out of his pocket and lit it. He went across the bridge. The display of watches was getting more distinct. He pressed against the window and saw the English, Arabic, and Japanese price tags on the watches. A cuckoo clock just struck nine. He walked into the shop.

"Sir, what can I do for you?" asked the assistant.

"I would like to buy the cuckoo clock," said Reeves.

"Which one, sir?"

"The one that just struck nine," said Reeves.

"Yes, sir, I will pack it for you."

Reeves picked up the package.

"Come again, sir."

"I will if I need another clock," Reeves smiled.

"Good day, sir."

Reeves walked out of the shop. He took the wrapping off and looked at the clock carefully. He walked into a telephone booth. He unscrewed the back of the clock and from among its innumerable components, he took out a sheet of folded paper. He read it for a while, put it in his pocket, and started dialing.

"We are in trouble," said Reeves softly into the mouthpiece.

"I hope it is big trouble. In Washington, it is 4:00 A.M. Anyway, shoot," said Gibson, the Chief, the Chief of the FBI.

"Stewart is dead."

"What? Who killed him?" Gibson got out of his bed and put the bed light on.

"Nobody, he died of viral encephalitis."

"What is that supposed to mean?" said the firm voice from Washington.

"Well, that's the bug infecting the brain," said Reeves.

"I know that. I mean how the hell did he die overnight? Are you sure the Red Bear did not squeeze him too hard?"

"Well, he took a girl to his room the night before. I just bought a cuckoo clock. Cuckoo says she is a call girl with no affiliations. She has no contact with Red Bear. She was in New York a couple of years ago. To be sure, we should check her background."

"All right, send her particulars through the urgent diplomatic pouch. But I still don't understand how you can trust the judgment of a single doctor. They make mistakes. They might pretend otherwise, but some of them are the most ignorant people I have seen," insinuated Gibson.

"But there were no signs of poisoning."

"Well, you are the man on the spot. I do not want any loose ends when you are finished there."

Said Reeves, "If he was squeezed by the Red Bear, I bet there is a parrot singing in your office in Washington. How otherwise would anyone know he was working for us?"

"Don't worry about that," said Gibson emphatically. "Leave it to me. I will get to his throat before he sings again. I hope you haven't already tripped the alarm. Be careful, your life could be in danger too. Do you need help?"

"No. I will yell if I need any help."

"Make sure you yell louder than Stewart did. Good luck."

Reeves put down the phone. He had tremendous respect for Gibson. Gibson was so stolid and pragmatic, always able to examine the pros and cons and options with such unattached scrutiny and then to guide his thoughts in a practical and unemotional manner toward a target, which he always defined so well.

Reeves knew there was enormous amount of business to be taken care of and as circumstances would dictate, he had to now take care of it single-handed. Moore was there, but then he was only a technical expert. He had no idea of the enormous angles of a mission so sensitive. Besides, he was running out of time. Two of the most important days had been spent with the events surrounding Stewart's death. Deep inside he knew the girl had poisoned Stewart, but proof was another story. Try and suggest anything to those doctors, they get defensive and think you are questioning their judgment. Gibson was probably right. Doctors, most of them, like to talk with conviction. This discourages questions from patients and their relatives, and besides this builds a halo of confidence around them. But their firm convictions are scientifically not always right.

Reeves also knew he was a sitting duck. The force that had eliminated Stewart could be directed against him in a thousand different ways. For his own sake, he had hoped that Gibson was wrong, the doctor was right, and his own logical evaluations were full of flaws.

Next morning, Reeves walked out of the hotel. A biting chill was still in the air. It was a dull, slow day. It was snowing heavily. But since the clouds had totally shrouded the sun and the sky all around, it gave an illusion of light snow, for there was no light reflected from the snowflakes. As he walked on the street, his head was damp with mushy snow that he could not shake off. He was walking at a faster pace, for the invisible snow was getting fiercer. He stopped and looked into a display window. Toward the right side, in his field of vision, he saw a tall man in a long gray coat, standing near the next shop. As he started to walk, the man leisurely came to the middle of the sidewalk. Reeves was sure he was being followed. The next moment Reeves spotted a cab pulling near the curb. As the passenger got out, Reeves jumped into the cab. He looked in the rear window of the cab. The man was crossing the road at a fast pace. As the cab sped, Reeves kept looking through the rear window. The man was nowhere in sight. He had lost him, but for how long?

Reeves placed the box containing the Sea Cola bottles back in the locker. That was the easy part. He removed the partition between the lockers and placed the box containing the Sea Cola bottles in its right place. He replaced the partition, and then he replaced the box containing the computer. The computer would automatically activate at 9:00 P.M. and cement the partition in its correct place. As he was walking out of the bank, he heard footsteps behind him.

"Just a minute, sir." Reeves heart galloped. He felt a cold sweat and lifeless feeling in his hands. There was only one alternative, that was to run out of the bank and get lost in the street.

"Sir, you forgot to sign," said the bank teller.

Reeves looked back.

"Over here, sir."

Reeves signed the paper. He kept his lips tight, but inside he was bursting with an enormous sense of relief. Now, as a matter of fact, he found this situation rather amusing. He was confident now. His pace was relaxed. The important part of this mission in Zurich was back on the track. As he walked out of the bank, he looked around. The man was nowhere in sight. The pavement was covered with snow. As he walked gingerly, he felt the spongy thrust of snow on his soles. As he crossed the road, the snow on the road was packed and he felt a little unsure on his feet. He walked into the shop.

"Excuse me. This cuckoo clock I bought yesterday doesn't work."

"I am sorry, sir. I will change it. Please step into the back of the shop."

Reeves followed the man.

"I need to know more about the girl," said Reeves.

"I told you she is clean," said the shop assistant.

"I am not totally convinced," said Reeves.

"All right, I will make some more enquiries."

"I have very little time. I think I was followed by a man today. I could be in danger."

As Reeves walked out of the shop, he knew in this spy paradise he was a helpless target. He looked around. His heart was pacing fast. The snow had faded to an occasional flake. The sun was peeping through a mountain of intense clouds. In this sudden surge of sunlight, he witnessed the fate of individual flakes. They were floating in the gentle wind, as they reached near the ground their to and fro movements became less distinct, and as they hit the ground, they melted immediately, merging with the dirty slush of salt and sand. Reeves walked at a leisurely pace. Water had soaked into his shoes, and he felt dampness in his socks. He curled his toes as if to dissipate the dampness; nothing different happened. He turned to the left side and entered the cafe. He sipped coffee and looked out of the window. The sun had disappeared again, choked by the clouds all around. How strange, he thought, this country Switzerland had been built on exploiting the negative features of the Free World and the Communist world. As long as there was conflict on this planet, and there always would be a conflict, this country would exploit people with its neutrality, a country whose morality was only based on the positive balance of its financial institutions. Here people had bargained their emotions and sense of reasoning to differentiate right from wrong for a bundle of Swiss francs.

CHAPTER 12

Jacobs walked briskly across the sidewalk to his waiting black Cadillac limousine. On this April day, spring was securely locked in place. The chill of the fading winter had left. It was replaced by a cool or warm feeling, depending upon what one was wearing. As Jacobs approached the limousine, the chauffeur opened the door.

"Mr. Jacobs, I am your new chauffeur, sir, until Anthony Boyle returns."

"Is Anthony on vacation?" asked Jacobs.

"No sir, he has illness in his family. I am Jim Reeves."

"Jim, to Kennedy Airport."

"Departures or Arrivals, sir?"

"Departures."

There was no illness in Anthony Boyle's family. The fact was that Mr. Williams, the president of the Sea Cola Corporation, had gotten increasingly concerned with the recent kidnappings of industrialists. With Jacobs completely negligent to any security, Mr. Williams's fears had compounded. Jacobs had refused to adhere to any guidelines of the security staff. "You are getting paranoid, you are overreacting," he had told them. But the president, Mr. Williams wasn't going to give up. He knew that any left-wing fanatic, or, for that matter, any anarchist group, could easily kidnap Jacobs and demand a couple of million dollars ransom. He wasn't about to take that chance. He would have preferred a more visible security, but when Jacobs declined that, Williams sought help from the FBI. The FBI put their own agent Jim Reeves in the driver's seat until things cooled off. They had wired the limousine so that there was direct communication with the FBI office. It was hot inside the limousine from the bright sun outside. Jacobs set the air conditioner at seventy degrees. As the limousine cruised along Second Avenue, Jacobs pushed the button on the arm rest. The glass partition between the front and back seat receded.

"Who is sick?" asked Jacobs.

"His wife, sir."

"Nice man. . . .Hope she is all right. Make it to be Pan Am Departures."

"Good luck with your speech, sir."

Jacobs folded the papers and placed them in his briefcase. There were two distinct worlds flourishing in this limousine, both worlds separated by a glass partition as effectively as if one world was a potential threat to the other's existence.

Jacobs was a keynote speaker at the Food Additives Conference in Chicago at 8:00 P.M. The American report that the additives in soft drinks may contribute toward cancer had generated a tremendous controversy. The food-processing companies had contradicted the report, and they had chosen Jacobs as their main defendant. The food industry was under fire from the consumer associations. They had accused the industry of causing cancer, kidney disease, heart disease, and allergies. In fact any disease that the medicine could not find the cause for, they had accused and laid the blame at the doorsteps of the food industry. Who else but Jacobs was the right choice to rebut these charges? Not only was he the vice-president of the biggest mineral-water plant, he sincerely believed in the product and had seen both sides of the story. After all, he had risen from the ranks. His speech was all ready. But ahead of him was a murky path. While the scientists look toward a controversy with the eagerness and inquisitiveness of a child, by the same measure the public at large hate sifting through contradictory evidence. It was left to Jacobs's skills to satisfy both. If not silence, it would certainly muffle the voice of opposition.

Traffic now had slowed down to a trickle. A nuclear freeze march was coming from the opposite direction. It was much bigger than the police had expected. It was being led by a Buddhist monk wearing a long saffron robe. This was the first year for the march, but considering its success, it was sure to become an annual event. Jacobs was becoming impatient. His flight was due in one hour. He looked back. There was a line of cars behind him as far as he could see. He pushed the button. The glass partition receded to the left.

"Jim, how big a parade is this?"

"I wouldn't worry, sir. We will be out of here in ten minutes."

The traffic had completely stopped.

"What the hell are these people wasting their time for? I bet each one of them is on government handout," said Jacobs. He lowered the electric window on the left side.

Jacobs got out of the car and stood on his toes to see how long a queue of cars was ahead of him.

A tall man, at least six feet tall, wearing a blue turtleneck sweater, got out of the Volkswagen Bug behind him.

"Shouldn't be long before you get out of this mess. Then you will have a whole new life ahead of you, " he said.

Jacobs looked around. Surely the man couldn't be talking to him, but he was. Everyone else was totally absorbed in the march. The man was standing so close to the open door of the car that Reeves could hear the conversation.

The man said, "Hey, man. I am talking to you. Your body is succulent with all the blood you have sucked. Now the time has come to see the Blue Vampire."

Jacobs smiled. There was no point in responding to this sort of talk.

Reeves turned his head back and said loudly, "Sir, Mr. Jacobs, what are you doing? Please get into the car."

Jacobs looked at the man. The man was smiling, his eyes fixed at Jacobs. He raised his eyebrows, eagerly awaiting Jacobs's response.

Reeves reinforced his request, "Mr. Jacobs. In the car please."

Reeves tried to open the door. The door would not budge an inch. There was a police officer standing there with his knee pressed against the door.

"Officer, your knee is in the way. I am trying to get out of the car," said Reeves through the open car window.

"I know that. I don't want you to get out," said the officer.

Jacobs was back in the car. The man followed him in.

Reeves was furious. Not only at the man but also at Jacobs. Why the hell did Jacobs have to get out of the car to look at the damn traffic? With his right hand at the gun, he turned around.

"Get out of the car or I'll blow your brains out," said Reeves to the man.

"Man, don't get hot. Mr. Jacobs is a businessman. He will understand. I will make him a business proposition. I am pointing a Magnum at him. One false move and you will be collecting his pieces from the road," he said sitting by the side of Jacobs. "Drop your gun on the floor."

Reeves hesitated a little. The man pushed his gun into Jacobs's ribs. In total despair, Jacobs looked at Reeves, "Do as he says."

Reeves dropped his gun on the floor.

"I tell you what. Supposing you move over and let the police officer take over the driving," said the man.

The march had passed by. Chilling silence had taken over. The fake police officer entered the car. He took his hat off and started to drive. He took the chauffeur's hat from Reeves's head and put it on his own head, "See, a hat can make a lot of difference. A minute ago, I was a trusted policeman, now I am authenticated chauffeur." He jerked the phone and ripped it off the dashboard. "We want complete privacy. Don't we?"

Jacobs looked at the man by his side. The barrel of the gun was still digging into his ribs.

The man handed Jacobs an envelope. "There is a message for you in there."

Reeves turned around, "I will take the ransom note."

He hit Reeves with the butt of the gun. "Place your damn hands over the dashboard. I will let you off this time. Try and make one more move and your brain will be sprawling over the windshield, like a Picasso painting."

Reeves saw a few stars floating around. When they disappeared he put his hands firmly against the dashboard. Reeves couldn't understand why Jacobs had to get out to survey the traffic jam. If only he had a little warning or inkling that Jacobs was going to get out, he would have never let him do that. The FBI had installed a panic button in the car. He never got a chance to push that either. When the man had followed Jacobs into the car, he thought the man must be spaced out on drugs or booze. But he was wrong. This was well organized. After all, that was the reason the FBI had put him in the driver's seat, so that he could keep a close eye on Jacobs. Too late now. Both were in for a long ordeal. Surely these people would barter Jacobs's head for at least a couple of million dollars. Why did Jacobs have to get out of the car?

The man in the turtleneck sweater spoke out, "I was wrong. I thought you people were civilized. I was hoping I don't have to resort to this . . . Mr. Jacobs, turn your back toward me and put your hands behind your back. He tied Jacobs's wrists together with an electric cord. "Now you, Federal Ass, put your hands behind you." He tied Reeves's wrists with an electric cord as well.

Jacobs looked at the man. "Please don't harm us. If you let me make one telephone call, I will arrange the ransom right away." Jacobs knew this was a desperate request. There was no way the man was going to agree to that.

Reeves interjected, "If you don't trust us, one of you can make the telephone call."

The man caught hold of a tuft of hair and yanked Reeves's neck off his shoulders.

"Man, I don't like you. If you are not careful, I will make you another police statistic. For the last time, I am warning you. Shut up or I will shut you up."

Reeves felt a prick in his shoulder. The man had injected a tranquilizer. Reeves sat there absolutely still. Obviously the man was panicky and impulsive. There was no point in provoking him further. One consolation was Jacobs that was holding out extremely well under the strain of this ordeal. The car turned into a multi-story parking garage. The noise of the surrounding automobiles had disappeared and was replaced by the nauseating stink of the exhaust fumes. He followed the yellow arrows to the third floor and turned into the C lane. The car was barely moving. He put the flashers on. Reeves was getting drowsy. His head slumped against the dashboard. The man pulled him back from his collar and ordered, "Sit up straight." Reeves heard the orders. He had neither ambition nor energy to respond. Except for regular movements of his chest muscles, he was still. The sedative was doing a fast job. Next moment he slumped against the side door.

As the car reached the end of the C lane, a white van pulled out of a parking space. A diminutive, bald man came out of the side door of the van. He handed an attaché case to the man wearing the turtleneck, sitting by the side of Jacobs.

He opened the attaché case and felt around. "Hope these are the right greens."

"Absolutely, one hundred thousand dollars. I take over from here."

Jacobs sat there calmly, absorbed in his own thoughts as though all these business transactions being done on his life were only of peripheral interest to him. The man may not have been so wrong, after all. Somehow he was going to get out of this mess. Guaranteed he had only few friends, but they were all in the right places. They would not abandon him.

The bald man held Jacobs by the arm and pushed him into the van. There was no point in resisting. Jacobs obliged with his hands tied behind him, wondering what sort of sedative they had given to his chauffeur. What would they do to him?

The man in the back of the limo asked, "What do I do with this Fed bum?"

"I leave that to your discretion," said the bald man. The van door closed, and it moved toward the exit sign.

The two men balanced Reeves behind the wheel, placed a newspaper in front of him, and walked toward the elevator leading to the street below.

CHAPTER 13

"Transit Flight 157, Airline Nicaragua, from Newark to Managua, Nicaragua. Please present your travel documents at Gate Twelve," said the muffled voice at the International Airport, Houston. Jacobs stood in the line, closely followed by the man who had accompanied him from Newark Airport. Jacobs had a short artificial mustache and short beard, which made a circular island around his mouth. He looked like a French salesman in search of untapped markets for Renaults.

Jacobs walked into the aircraft. There was nothing else he could do. He had to play the game according to the rules set by others. That made him uneasy. He had always been in control of his destiny. But now the circumstances had changed. There was nothing else he could do except wait and see. One wrong move and his life could turn into dust right in front of his eyes. The man who had accompanied him from Newark Airport had assured him that if he played the game right, nothing would go wrong. But he had also warned Jacobs that at the least suspicion that things were not going well, he would pull the gun and hijack the aircraft. How the man had managed to bring the gun across the airport security checkpoint at Newark, Jacobs had no idea. He was sitting next to Jacobs. Jacobs was convinced that he meant business and had his finger at the trigger all the time. But somehow he knew he was going to make it. Hard work, destiny, and planning were all on his side.

The jet had completed its assault on the motionless clouds and emerged on the top. Jacobs looked out. Far away there was a brilliantly shining star. Close to it there was another star that looked pale in contrast. He kept looking at them and saw another one close by, which waxed and waned. He wasn't sure whether this was another star or product of his imagination. To be sure, he narrowed his eyes to concentrate. The twinkling kept on. Then he lost it all, for the aircraft had taken a turn and was headed to Managua. The "No Smoking" sign had disappeared. Then he heard a squeaky voice. He had to strain his ears to understand it.

"Ladies and gentlemen, this is Captain Revalo. Right now we are flying at an altitude of 35,000 feet at a speed of 600 miles per hour. Next stop is Managua, Nicaragua. Flying time is two hours and fifteen minutes. Thank you."

Jacobs pushed the button on the arm rest and eased into a reclining position. He tried to relax with his eyes closed, but there was too much excitement and uncertainty pent up within him.

"Sir, dinner will be served soon. Would you like a cocktail?"

"Please. Vodka martini."

Perhaps half of his life had been spent in air travel. But for the first time, he was witnessing the world behind the closed curtains of the first-class cabin. He had always traveled first class, where expensive champagnes, caviars, and attention of air stewardesses outdid each other. If he wanted to discuss business, he could do it as easily as in his office. But today, not out of choice, he was traveling in tourist class. Here the passengers were not wearing designer clothes. They were wearing jeans, slacks, T-shirts, and sneakers. But there was something endearing about them. They were sitting there unabashedly, staring at the stewardesses, minding everyone else's business, and expanding their acquaintance horizons. One of the passengers had taken off his shoes and was dangling his feet in the aisle. The color of the socks had faded and fibers had frayed from a million tumbles in the washing machine. This wasn't the world he was used to. He was always surrounded by the rich and the powerful. But today he had no choice. Perhaps right now this was the safest place for him.

"Your dinner, sir," said the stewardess.

"Could I have another drink, please? Same as the last."

The man sitting by his side was going to take care of him during his flight. Jacobs looked at him momentarily. He said nothing. There was no need to. Question was written all over his face.

The man kept his hand in his pocket, close to his gun. With his left hand, he gently tapped Jacobs's shoulder. There was sincere assurance in his eyes. The jet sounded like a million gallons of water rushing down a steep waterfall. He barely raised his voice above the jet sound.

"I won't use the gun unless I have to," he said. "Just stick to the plan as we discussed."

But in times like these, who could stick to any plans? An air marshall could sneak behind him and pump a bullet into his back. An air stewardess could drug the drinks and in a matter of minutes they could turn up into a heap of waste and then all would be over. But worst still, a struggle could start, bullets flying all over, and one could go astray. In a matter of moments, his dreams could be over. He knew his fellow passenger was cool and confident, but then when suddenly mortal disaster is thrust into one's face, one had to fall back on instinct, which, after all, is a matter of playing odds devoid of logic.

"Ladies and gentlemen," said the captain, "We are flying over the Gulf of Mexico. We have just crossed the international border between United States and Mexico."

Jacobs wished Chimanski were alive that day, although he would not understand the complexities of the world, for his world only existed within the confines of the hospital. He had no perspective of the world. His morals, his ethics, and his style were all shaped by the medical environment, perhaps some influence from the Jewish religion. A smile had appeared on Jacobs's face when he thought of Chimanski's girl friend. Certainly ridiculous. Sincere, yes. Imagine him thinking he had searched for this girl for centuries. The fact was the bastard was too immature and infatuated by this girl, to a level bordering on insanity. He could not understand how a man so intelligent and gifted could believe in such abstracts as God, love, and life after death. But he admired Chimanski's simplicity and subtleness. Everything he said, when he was alive, carried so little weight.

At that particular time, everything had seemed so unimportant, but now as the time had passed, his words had strangely picked up tremendous momentum. Perhaps his love for Judy wasn't so silly after all. Maybe it had more depth than he had perceived. Maybe it wasn't simple infatuation, for Chimanski wasn't a man of spontaneous emotional displays. He was a deeper man. All his life he spent in giving all he had to his patients. Perhaps in Judy, he perceived a depth of concern and sense of giving that even surpassed his own. He remembered his own hospitalization and Chimanski's visits. Chimanski exhibited the combination of energy and enthusiasm of a child combined with a wisdom of mature age. The two blended in a subtle manner. Even after his death, Chimanski continued to have a strange impact on him, not so much as a change in his views, but rather like a dent on his conscience. But Jacobs's convictions were logical and not subject to emotions. He knew emotions were the weakest link between man and his goals. Incidentally, that might have been the weakest part in Chimanski's life. He had wisdom, intelligence, and a sense of timing, but all this sabotaged by poor qualities like compassion, love, and emotions, weaknesses that prevented him from exerting maximum impact on this earth. As far as he himself was concerned, except for minor deviations, he would not be caught with those weaknesses. He was linked to the future with steel bonds, like ruthlessness and dedication to a purpose. Human beings, with their fragile displays, had no place in his world. They were expendable.

"Sir, would you like a blanket?" asked the stewardess.

"No, thanks."

Jacobs looked at her. Her smile was factitious and forced. Her eyes reflected shallowness. He thought of Chimanski again. There was nothing artificial about him. His anger, his smile, and his concerns were all real. Certainly subtle, but so real. With him he knew where he was. No wonder his patients had such confidence in him. It had been only a couple of months when

Jacobs had invited Chimanski to his weekend estate in the Mohawk Valley. After a couple of hours of skiing, he had taken him to his favorite restaurant and had asked, "Olig, how close was it when I was brought to the emergency room?"

"I don't know. Only God can answer that question. But you were very sick," said Chimanski in a matter-of-fact voice.

"You are a man of science. You certainly don't believe in God."

"I certainly do," persisted Chimanski.

"You mean you believe in God and its various ramifications?" Jacobs appeared more agitated than surprised.

Chimanski asked, "What ramifications?"

Jacobs moved forward and put his hands on the table, "You know what I mean. Hell, heaven, various prizes and punishments, promises of life after death."

Chimanski was a little surprised at the seriousness with which Jacobs was pursuing the conversation. He tried to play down with humor. "As an expert on death, I say no, but as an amateur, I say there is life after death."

"In other words you are afraid to commit," Jacobs pressed him further.

"I am merely expressing a dilemma that constantly hounds a scientist with religion. What is your philosophy anyway?" asked Chimanski.

Jacobs had repositioned himself in the chair. The ball was back in his court. "I have no philosophy. History of mankind tells me that after our biological existence ceases, that's the end of it."

Chimanski smiled, "Tell me. Why are we indulging in luxuries of death and life thereafter?"

Jacobs laughed. "I find the subject fascinating."

"You probably wouldn't find it fascinating if you dealt with life and death every day," responded Chimanski.

"For example, let's take another angle. If you were to die tomorrow, would you be quietly relaxing and fantasizing about life after death or would you be rushing around frantically to fulfill your last wish here on this earth?"

Chimanski exploded into laughter. "Will you stop asking silly questions? . . . That's the whole beauty of this concept of God. Till the very last breath, we never know the end has come."

Jacobs persisted, "Supposing we take a hypothetical situation that the end is tomorrow?"

Chimanski asked, "Do you know something that I don't know?"

"No. I just find instantaneous human thinking against positively fatalistic odds, fascinating."

Chimanski shook his head from side to side. "Let me see. Let me get this question right, since it seems to be overwhelmingly fascinating to you. You mean if I know I am going to die tomorrow, what's the only thing I would like to do before I am mortally struck?"

Jacobs, "You got it."

"I suppose you ask a silly hypothetical question and an equally silly hypothetical answer is what you get. Well, I met this girl about six weeks ago. She is beautiful and charming, but there is something more than that. I have a feeling I have searched for her for centuries. Of that I am absolutely positive. I have battled with this feeling ever since. It as as if it's not her, but the theory is more important. The theory is that we have searched for each other for centuries, and I feel confident that we were set up for each other by some unknown force. So if I have to die tomorrow, I will certainly let her know of this strange phenomenon. It seems stupid, I know. Yet it is so true."

Jacobs, "Fascinating. But all baloney. Or you can call it infatuation. Surely, you are a scientist. You don't believe in this mumbo-jumbo."

Replied Chimanski, "I suppose you are right. Still it is fascinating. But remember all theories are pure baloney when put forward first."

"You know very well that all romances are made in heaven, but effectively destroyed on this earth. Right now you are in the heavenly phase."

Chimanski smiled, "What are you? Some sort of authority on romance and its various ramifications?"

Jacobs started laughing. He looked out of the window at the Mohawk River. "Look at the river, completely choked by big slabs of ice. It happens every year when the weather warms up a little. This year the January thaw did it."

"Ladies and gentlemen, we are passing through a wind turmoil. Please fasten your safety belts."

Jacobs put on his seat belt. He was completely exhausted, mentally and physically. Thoughts entering his brain were so sporadic and confusing that he wished he could go to sleep. He put the light out and pushed the seat into a reclining position. The aircraft was passing through rough winds. Through the window he saw the lightning, which appeared so unusual because he could not hear the accompanying thunder. The movie was halfway through. Jacobs had paid no attention to that. Suddenly the aircraft sunk down, and it felt as if it was going to hit the core of the universe. The casualness of the stewardesses as they moved around was reassuring that there was nothing drastically wrong. The aircraft leveled off again.

An hour later he got up, awakened by a tap on his shoulder by the man sitting next to him. He heard the squeaky voice again.

"Ladies and gentlement, please fasten your safety belts. We are about to descend. We are approaching Managua. It is 3:00 A.M. in Managua, local time. Temperature at the airport is 66°F. Please remain seated until the aircraft comes to a complete stop. Thank you."

Jacobs still felt exhausted. The mission of his life was complete. There was no force either in heaven or hell that had the power to stop the machinery he had set in motion. A sudden surge of joy erupted inside him. The volcano inside him, which had been subdued for years and years, had finally erupted. Up to now a thousand things could have gone wrong. As a matter of fact, they did. But he was a man who had a firm grip on the handle of life. He had finally steered the mission to a complete success. While the world around would crumble, he would deserve a well-deserved vacation from years of planning and hard work.

CHAPTER 14

Nicaragua was in political turmoil. There was almost complete control by Communists. Jacobs got out of the aircraft onto the conduit leading to the airport. He felt a little out of place, nevertheless, relaxed. Most of the passengers were talking in Spanish in a subdued tone. He had only taken a few steps when he saw a sloppily dressed military man with an automatic weapon hanging from his shoulder. His finger was on the trigger. The man was saying something softly periodically in Spanish. His soft speech betrayed his tough appearance. Jacobs took the turn along with the crowd of passengers. Ahead of him was a long corridor at the end of which there was an arrow pointing to the left, with "Customs" written in English and Spanish.

"The airport has changed a lot from what I remember," said someone from the flowing crowd.

"Excuse me, Mr. Jacobs?"

Jacobs suddenly stopped and turned his head to the left. There was a man in a light-blue uniform with a black cap. There was a red star in the middle of the front of the cap. The man obviously spoke with an accent. He displayed absolutely certainty. Still, Jacobs tried to dodge the question.

"I don't think I know you," said Jacobs.

"That's not important. Follow me, please," said the man, as he started walking toward the side door.

Jacobs followed the man into a large room, while the rest of the passengers kept walking straight ahead. The man opened the door and led him into another room, with a deep blue carpet.

As Jacobs entered the room, he saw a man sitting in a military khaki uniform behind the table. Instantaneously the man got up and galloped toward Jacobs, almost tripping as he was going around the table. As he approached Jacobs, he caught hold of his hand and started shaking it briskly.

"Welcome to Nicaragua." He looked at Jacobs and discovered that Jacobs wasn't particularly enthusiastic. Jacobs sat on the sofa chair while the man slowly walked back to his chair behind the table.

"How was your journey, sir?" he asked.

"Okay. I would like to talk to Mr. Rodrigues. I have his telephone number," said Jacobs.

"He left a message for you, sir. He is expecting you. He is delayed at the ministry."

"Fine. I will wait around here."

Jacobs looked around the room. Right above where the man was sitting, there was a large portrait of a man in a military uniform, with numerous medals decorating both his chest pockets. Jacobs looked carefully. There was no name written underneath. Jacobs thought this portrait was unusually large, considering the height of the wall.

The man behind the table was busy flipping pages and pages of documents, scribbling comments here and there, and frequently looking straight ahead into empty space and surveying Jacobs in his field of vision. Jacobs noticed that the table was obviously made with careful attention to details. There was an empty cup of coffee lying on it, and close by there were circular marks from hot cups placed there in the past. It was obvious to him that the man and the table were not made for each other. He looked at the legs. They were still in perfect shape.

"How long before I can see Mr. Rodrigues?" Jacobs made sure he separated each word.

"He said about one half-hour, sir."

"How is the revolution?" asked Jacobs.

"Good. Some obstacles. Comrade Rodrigues is one of our chief architects."

"I know he is brilliant," said Jacobs.

"Brilliant and passionately committed to the revolution."
He practically chewed up the word passionately and distorted
it beyond such recognition that it took a while for Jacobs to
realize what he had said. .

"What is his position?" Jacobs lighted his pipe.

"Minister of Internal Affairs."

This time Jacobs was ready, and he was listening with a
devotional intensity. He was determined to understand in spite
of the man's accentual distortion of the words. The man also
had noticed the strain his accent had imposed on Jacobs, and
this time was separating each word, augumenting them with
hand gestures.

Misreading the blank expression on Jacobs's face, he re-
phrased his answer, "Looks after the home affairs."

Jacobs smiled and apologized for the difficulty in understanding him. This broke the barrier between them, which Jacobs
had unnecessarily raised himself. There was no need to play
any games. He had to change his life-style, learn to trust people,
learn to relax, and have a general friendship with people around.

"The coffee was delicious. What's your job?"

"I am Chief of Security at the airport. My name is Juan
Garcia."

"Mr. Garcia, I was a little unfriendly when I met you at first,
all due to a particular circumstance. How do you say 'Mister' in
Spanish?" Jacobs was demolishing the barrier.

"Señor." His eyes were slightly damp from emotions. A
sparkled had appeared in them, "Señor Jacoooooooobs, I understand."

Jacobs burst into laughter. No one before had stretched
his name to such limits.

The telephone rang. Garcia picked up the phone. His relaxed
expression instantaneously evaporated.

"Comrade Rodrigues is on his way," he announced.

He briskly stood up. He was rubbing his hands together.

"Maybe I should meet him in the main lobby. Maybe he
wants me to stay with you," he said with a detectable tremble
in his voice.

Jacobs looked at Garcia with his eyebrows raised. He could not understand what the fuss was all about.

Garcia's sixth sense picked up the question. "Mr. Rodrigues does not tolerate any flaws."

Jacobs realized he was in a completely different world now where hierarchy ruled ruthlessly. Here man's ego created a lust for power beyond question, which corrupted the most innocent of men in the political systems. Garcia's reaction to Rodrigues was a reflection of such threat. Garcia heard approaching footsteps outside the door. He leaped toward the door. Before he could reach it, the door was flung wide open with force. Rodrigues looked at Jacobs for a second or two. If he smiled, it wasn't evident through his bushy, rather substantial mustache.

"Comrade Jacobs. Welcome to Nicaragua." Rodrigues shook his hand firmly and embraced him.

"Thanks. It's wonderful to be here."

"You picked the right time. History is being made here." Rodrigues was obviously proud of what was going on in Nicaragua.

"I know you are the giant among the history makers," complimented Jacobs.

Rodrigues smiled and looked at Garcia with his piercing black eyes. He pointed his finger at him, "I will call you when I need you."

Rodrigues was a slim man of a medium height. He was in his thirties, with a suntan complexion.

As Garcia left the room, Rodrigues poured coffee for himself and Jacobs.

"Any problem on the way?" asked Rodrigues.

"None so far."

Rodrigues pulled the chair next to Jacobs, "Moscow has been on my back since you left Newark."

"Who in Moscow?" asked Jacobs.

Rodrigues smiled, "Who else? Zerenkov, of course."

"Let me talk to him."

"You will in time. You have to understand, our revolution is not complete yet. We are still not in absolute control. I have to be very careful. I cannot afford any risks."

"What risks? I will send him a coded message." Jacobs, who up to now was talking in a placid tone, was visibly irritated.

"I know how you feel, but I have a bigger responsibility. The security of Nicaragua. Any indication that you are here could bring in CIA interference, and that's the last thing I need at the present time."

Jacobs was furious. He suddenly got up. "I just don't believe it. It's insanity. I got to talk to him directly. Supersensitive material. You could risk a leak through dubious channels."

"Jacobs, don't lose your sense of reasoning in a fit of anger."

Jacobs thought that was even more insulting.

"Jacobs," continued Rodrigues, after a short pause and broad smile, "let me explain. We have this highly reliable contact in the German embassy. Get this clear. This source is personally approved by Zerenkov. Very reliable. Highly tested source, never any leak." Rodrigues stood up straight from the table against which he was leaning and passed on a drink to Jacobs. Jacobs kept staring at the table, appreciating its exquisite design. He was somewhat annoyed at the contempt with which Garcia and Rodrigues were treating this piece of art.

Jacobs was subdued now. "I don't know. It's unbelievable."

Rodrigues momentarily looked at Jacobs. He nodded. It was difficult to interpret whether it was out of agreement or understandable difference of opinion.

"Comrade Rodrigues, are you sure about this man, his credentials?"

"Absolutely. Zerenkov thinks he is all right, and you know what that means."

"Well, how do we send the message?" asked Jacobs.

"You give me the message and I will pass it along. Better before he goes to the embassy."

"I suppose it will be coded." Jacobs knew it wasn't a good suggestion to a security minister.

Rodrigues laughed. "Absolutely."

Jacobs thought for a while. "If you don't mind, I would rather wait a little longer."

"That's fine with me. But remember, I do not have security clearance for you from Moscow. I have to wait until I get a reply to my message to New York to give you security clearance."

Jacobs abruptly got up from the chair and thumped his drink on the table. "That's absolutely ridiculous. You know who I am."

"Comrade Jacobs. I am not interested in your opinion of my security arrangement. Let's get one thing absolutely clear. I make the rules of the game here. You play accordingly or you don't play at all. Your government asked me to give you protection. I have already sent a message to the Soviet embassy in New York. At any moment now, we will be getting confirmation on your identity." Rodrigues swallowed the rest of his drink in one swallow. "Now let's stop playing games and get the message to Moscow."

Jacobs was looking at Rodrigues, focusing more on his face, rather than his eyes, like a small child who knows he has been rebuked, rightly.

"Who did you contact in New York?" asked Jacobs.

Rodrigues smiled, "Who else? Your contact man in New York, Andrea Suchlov."

Jacobs lit his pipe. "So you know Suchlov."

"Sure I know him. I met him in Moscow when he was working for Zerenkov. Who do you think trained me in revolution? Zerenkov himself."

Jacobs couldn't pass the temptation. "How come Zerenkov never mentioned your name to me?"

"I suppose that's how he stays the Chief of KGB, the art of keeping many secrets."

Jacobs pressed him further. "All right, tell me, what's his code name?"

"Blue Vampire," said Rodrigues.

Jacobs burst into laughter. "How long have you known him? Sucks only blue blood."

"Long enough. We will discuss it when we reach home."

"I think we can talk business. This message has to be exact. This will set in motion the most intricately designed conspiracy." Jacobs pulled out a small diary from his pocket, tore a leaf out, wrote a coded message, and handed it over to Rodrigues.

Rodrigues took care of the message right away. He was rather relieved that Jacobs had mellowed considerably. His task from here onward would be easy. Jacobs felt secure. After all, Rodrigues exhibited a combination of authority, understanding, and a sense of direction. Besides, he had such inside information of Moscow, especially Zerenkov. He knew when he got back to Moscow, it would help him to know what strings to pull and when to pull them. He had lived in the capitalistic society so long he had forgotten the basic practicalities of communism. Rodrigues could certainly, if he played his cards right, bring him up to date. He knew, in spite of his achievements, he had to struggle when he got back to Moscow. To get any political power, the right time to start gathering information was now.

Rodrigues busied himself making telephone calls and giving orders with such authority that Jacobs was impressed. He had just put the phone down.

"How did you like Moscow?" asked Jacobs.

"Let me make the last telephone call. I will be with you in a minute."

Rodrigues was looking downward with intense concentration, which Jacobs had temporarily interrupted. His sudden arrival in Nicaragua had upset the minister's routine. After all, there were many loose ends to be tied. And as minister of internal affairs, Rodrigues had tremendous responsibility. There were more than pockets of resistance, which Rodrigues was systematically, yet ruthlessly, destroying. In that respect, he was Jacobs's kind of man. The look of intensity vanished from Rodrigues's face and was replaced by a cool and casual look as he got up from his chair and walked toward Jacobs.

"The best of my life. That's what I had in Moscow." He sat down on the chair next to Jacobs and continued, "To rub shoulders with revolutionaries from all over the world, I tell you, that's an experience."

"How is the revolution going on here?" asked Jacobs.

"Not too bad. People weren't prepared here, but that should be no problem. With the military behind us, we will thrust Communism down their throats."

"Do you think Uncle Sam will interfere?" asked Jacobs.

The casual expression on Rodrigues's face had changed into one of bitterness and anger. "Yes, the damn Uncle Sam. That's our greatest problem."

Jacobs got up from the chair. He emptied his pipe and started filling it with fresh tobacco.

"Try these from Cuba." Rodrigues handed him a cigar.

Jacobs smiled, "Uncle Sam may not be a problem to you anymore, for they will have unbelievable problems of their own soon enough."

"I know you did a great job. We should expect chaos in three weeks."

Jacobs, who was puffing on his freshly lit cigar, forcibly took the cigar out of his mouth, crushing the tobacco leaves with his teeth.

"How the hell do you know all this?"

"Sit down, Jacobs. Zerenkov told me all about your mission."

Jacobs slumped into the chair, sprawling all over. He took a deep breath and slowly let it out. "I just don't believe all this." He shook his head in disgust or dismay. "I was told my mission was top secret. Half the Communist world knows it; the other half is probably guessing it right."

Rodrigues was looking straight ahead at Jacobs. "You certainly don't believe you can bring about the revolution all alone. We are all partners. He told me all about your little trips to Switzerland."

Jacobs wasn't listening. He was still recovering from the shock of what Rodrigues had disclosed earlier.

"I just don't believe it. I was told it was the most guarded secret," said Jacobs.

"Sure it is a jealously guarded secret. You will understand when you realize how the system works. Among the top echelons of revolutionaries, there are no secrets. After all, it is an international movement. For example, if you failed, Zerenkov had a contingency plan."

"What plan?" asked Jacobs.

"How do I know? He never spelled out the details."

Rodrigues got up and carelessly tapped his cigar, dropping

the ashes in the ashtray but mostly on the table.

"How long have you known about this?" asked Jacobs.

"Remember when you were shot?" Rodrigues let out a laugh. "Since then. Zerenkov spent three nervous days in Managua then."

Jacobs was irritated, "That wasn't funny. I almost died, but for Dr. Chimanski who saved my life."

"And in gratitude, you almost jeopardized your mission."

Jacobs was furious. "You know, that's absurd. I suppose the same old source gave you that information."

Rodrigues stared ahead and took a deep puff at his cigar.

"What are we waiting for at the airport?" asked Jacobs.

"Comrade, I run a tight ship. In my philosophy, there is no place for slips, for the slips have their own way of turning into mistakes. Mistakes, when compounded, turn into blunders and when that happens, catastrophe is just around the corner. I must know who you are beyond any imaginable doubt. We have been tricked by the CIA before. If you are the real Jacobs, we will protect you. If you are not, I shall personally eliminate you shortly."

"Take your time to establish my identity because I want to stick around for a while," Jacobs smiled.

Rodrigues poured another drink for Jacobs.

"I am glad you like your victims well hydrated," said Jacobs.

Rodrigues exploded into laughter, interspersed with brief periods of cough, "I know how you feel. I cannot afford a slip."

"How's the weather outside?"

"Hot and sticky."

"Do you think that the CIA knows I am here?" asked Jacobs.

"I don't think so. The last I heard, Sea Cola Corporation is arranging for your ransom. That was a brilliant ploy by Zerenkov."

"Unbelievable. He had the FBI and CIA both on a short leash."

Jacobs showed no emotions. "But still there is a lot to be done."

"That's your problem and Zerenkov's. I will help but I will

not take the responsibility. I have enough headaches of my own," replied Rodrigues.

"I know." Jacobs thought that comment was uncalled for. He was the last man he would turn to for help if needed.

"Jacobs, would you kill a man in cold blood if you had the slightest doubt that your mission was in jeopardy?"

"I don't know what you are talking about."

"I am merely discussing it from a philosophical point of view. For example, I have no qualms about eliminating anyone I have doubts about."

"I suppose it's only a matter of degree."

Jacobs was pondering why this conversation was turning philosophical.

"Everything in life is a matter of degree. Depends upon where you draw the line. Zerenkov thinks you get emotionally involved with people, and when the time comes to make a rational decision, those attachments cloud your judgment."

"That's inaccurate . . . That's absurd. I have my own share of mistakes. But when anyone got too close to my mission, I took care of them, didn't I?"

Jacobs was trying to suppress an enormous anger and frustration building up inside. He was staying calm. After all, this was a man's personal opinion.

"But I think that doctor, what was his name, got too close to your mission," Rodrigues needled him further.

"You are drawing wild conclusions. That doctor was too much occupied with his work and his romance. As fate would have it, he was slowly pulled from the periphery to the center where the action was. I tried to stop him. I couldn't. I shut him up forever, didn't I? After all, he saved my life and besides, he was a fine doctor."

Rodrigues poured himself another drink. "That's where we differ. There are no fine doctors, engineers, or architects. In my reckoning there are only fine Communists. Out of curiosity, why did you kill the girl? Was it out of jealousy?"

Jacobs got up from the chair and put his glass on the table. He looked at Rodrigues as if he was going to chew him up and spit him out.

"Jealousy for what?" he said.

"I don't know. Either jealousy of the girl or the doctor. Depends upon with whom you were sexually involved."

Jacobs's heart was pounding inside his chest, but he remained calm. "Your inquiry is so degrading that I wouldn't dignify it with an answer."

"Comrade Jacobs, you are mistaken. It is not to satisfy my curiosity. It is Zerenkov who is so particular about details."

Jacobs replied, "When Zerenkov wants to know, I will tell him. In the meantime, you can continue your wild imaginations."

"Jacobs, you don't follow me. When I contact Zerenkov, he will expect complete details, which I can understand. After all, he sits in Kremlin making espionage decisions all over the world, and he needs all the information he can lay his hands on."

"All right, I will tell you." Jacobs realized there was no point in hiding this information, for Rodrigues already knew all about the mission. "After I shot Chimanski with a silencer attached to the gun, I was getting out of the apartment. The girl was screaming for a towel. I wanted a few minutes to get out of the apartment building. I opened the bathroom door a little and handed her the towel. Thinking me Chimanski, she grabbed hold of my arm in a passionate gesture and said something. I withdrew my arm abruptly, her nails accidentally scratched my arm. When I reached home, I realized that if she knew the assailant's arm had been scratched, she would pass this information to the police. There was always a possibility that the police could establish a link with me from the blood under her nails. I know it was a farfetched precaution. But do you think I had any choice? Besides, I had orders from Zerenkov not to leave any clues behind."

"Oh. I am not making any judgments. I think you were right. Besides, that shifted the blame to her husband."

Rodrigues walked back to the chair. He inclined back and kept flopping his hands in midair, playing around with the Cuban cigar between his teeth.

The telephone rang. He picked up the phone.

"I will take it here," said Rodrigues.

The man on the end said, "Is he with you?"

"Yes, Comrade Zerenkov. He is right here."

"How is he?" asked Zerenkov.

"A little shaken, but he is all right."

"I want you to give him the best protection you have."

"Leave it to me, Comrade. I will take care of him," Rodrigues smiled.

"Put him on," said the monotonous voice on the other side. "You stay on the phone as well."

Rodrigues gave Jacobs the phone. He went into the next room and picked up the extension phone.

"Welcome back. You did one marvellous job. Your code," said Zerenkov.

"Real thing." Jacobs was straining his ears to identify the voice on the other end of the phone. "Your code, Comrade."

"Blue Vampire. Your last mission?" asked Zerenkov.

"Operation Python in Czechoslovakia."

"Rodrigues, are you listening? He is the right man. Give him the best protection. He goes underground right away. They may be on his tail."

Jacobs intercepted, "When do I get home?"

The voice on the other side was still monotonous. "When the chaos starts. Not right now."

"What about phase two?" Jacobs's hands were drenched with sweat.

"Rodrigues takes over from here. I know he has problems. I have already sent him help."

"How can he take over a mission about which he does not know anything?" protested Jacobs.

"Leave that decision to me. Rodrigues has the coded names. Give him the key to the code." The voice on the other side had lost its monotonous quality. Now it was commanding. Jacobs was trying to speak, but the voice continued, "We will have to recode those names."

"Yes, Comrade, I will take care," said Rodrigues.

"That is absolutely crazy," insisted Jacobs.

"That's an order." The voice on the other side was so loud that Jacobs thought it was going to perforate his eardrum. "Rodrigues, I am sending help to keep the mission rolling."

"Yes, Comrade. I will take care until I receive further instructions from you," said Rodrigues.

"Rodrigues, over here we appreciate what you are doing for us. He goes underground from the airport."

The phone went dead. Rodrigues walked into the room. Jacobs was still holding the phone, partly recovered from the shock of the abrupt change of plans. But what did it matter now? He had already accomplished the main event of the mission.

Jacobs explained, "Comrade, I meant no insult to you when I protested against your taking over the mission."

"I understand, but remember, no one can forecast the future. Adjustments have to be made when things don't go as planned. If you don't go underground, you could be as safe as a sitting duck."

"I know but something doesn't seem right here."

"Well, I don't know; I trust Zerenkov's judgment. I leave you for fifteen minutes. After that we will leave the airport and for a few days you will have a chance to enjoy the Nicaraguan hospitality."

Rodrigues handed him the coded names and walked out of the room. Jacobs busied himself decoding those names as instructed by Zerenkov.

All his life he had spent for this moment of triumph. It had been an obstacle race, but now he had crossed the last hurdle, his feet securely back on the ground. He had put all the energy he had into those last few moments, and the ribbon was within his grasp. His energy wasn't muscle power. It was brain power that had been disciplined to intrigue, improvise, and beyond everything else, to scrutinize even the most trivial information so that his mission never got deflected.

Rodrigues was going to take over his mission to complete phase two. At least he would have the opportunity to discuss his work openly with him. The last five years he had spent in maddening loneliness. He could not trust anyone. He had to make all the decisions single-handed. After all, that's where lay the germs of success of his work. He knew if he had the option of discussion, his mission would have been doomed long ago. Everyone carried a price tag. In this business you could not look for a sale. You got only one chance. Merchandise may not be up to standard; everything could collapse in a short while, like a house of cards. Besides, at the last moment, people do get cold feet when persuaded to swim against the stream. He was different. He enjoyed swimming against the stream.

He wished the whole world would perform like a ballet, the whole wisdom of centuries concentrated in an assimilable form. People could think alike and be regimented into a uniform society. Different social and political systems were a disgrace to this earth. The United States was the worst culprit. People were thinking and moving in different directions. The poor man was thinking how to get rich, the rich man was wondering how to buy nirvana. It was a constant turmoil. People had no right to do and think whatever they liked. They were messing up this planet. The whole planet had to perform like a disciplined ballet so that all of us got a clear and purposeful message.

Destructive force I have unleashed will propagate itself, destroying all who deserve to be destroyed and preserving the chosen few. Undoubtedly, initially, there will be some blunders, but at least we will be marching in the right direction. Then a new order will emerge in this world. From ashes shall emerge a new world where there will be consensus of opinion with no dissensions. Socialism will then sweep in this world; then we will bury God forever.

If there was a man with logic, convictions, and sense of direction, that was Mr. Mullinkolv, the Chairman of Russia. Jacobs had met him six weeks earlier in his office in Kremlin.

Jacobs had asked, "Chairman Mullinkolv, I have a few questions regarding my mission."

"Yes."

"Did you personally approve of this?"

"Yes."

"I just wanted to be sure," said Jacobs.

"I think it was wise of you to double-check."

"You know the casualties are going to be in the millions."

Mullinkolv got up from his chair and walked to the window overlooking the Red Square. "Comrade, you know, we both have similar philosophies. You have read Karl Marx. You have read Lenin. Individuals have no meaning. Millions have no rights. Only community has rights."

"Your SALT II agreement with U.S.A. Aren't you accommodating with capitalism?" asked Jacobs.

Mullinkolv showed no emotions. His face was carved out of a stone, every wrinkle and every furrow meant to be permanent.

"Compromise never. Intrigues, yes. We are committed to revolution. Democracies are committed to evolution. Treaties are not worth the paper they are written on. Do you think I will compromise the revolution for a damn piece of paper?" His voice became high pitched, but still the stony face showed no change in its structure. "Of course millions will die. That's what we want, chaos in the U.S.A. Chaos, frustrations, miseries, all perfect ingredients for revolution. And you have the perfect recipe for all this. Once the chaos starts, we already have the nuclei of revolution in the free world. They know how to compound miseries. We have no gods, we have no religion, we have no faith, we have no morals, no principles, we are only committed to socialism. Now you understand the significance of SALT II? In an election year, any U.S president will walk over his mother's grave to get a few extra votes. So you see, SALT II gives him exactly that and a false sense of security. We still retain our destructive revolutionary policies," Mullinkolv continued his lecture on the virtues of communism.

"Son, I understand your dilemma. But you must know we cannot win against bourgeois free society, militarily or economically. So long as people were starving in this country, they were clinging to socialism. Now false intellectuals want more. They want expression. They want material benefits. The problem is they compare themselves with the bourgeois world. That's where you come in. You have to shatter that comparison. Of course millions will die. That's the whole idea. It will make World War II casualties look like Russian roulette gone sour. Son, we are proud of you. You are about to make an unsurpassable contribution to socialism."

For a while there was complete silence in the room.

Then Mullinkolv continued, "Now we are running out of time. We cannot control people with the big stick for too long. Individualism is creeping back into our society. Soon these individuals will feel suffocated. That is my greatest concern. There is nothing more dangerous than a suffocated man. He has nothing more left to lose. He has such tremendous energy to break open for a breath of fresh air. America gives him that promise of fresh air. You can destroy that forever and convert it into a stink so that the whole world realizes that there is only one viable system. Then communism will be forever embedded on this planet."

If Jacobs had any more questions, Mullinkolv had already answered them. Mullinkolv, he thought, possessed an extraordinary talent for perception of depth to look beyond the obvious.

Jacobs walked out of the Kremlin at eleven o'clock. There were few people walking around in Red Square. It was an unusually warm day for March in Moscow. The sun, through a veil of clouds, was a polished silver disk, reminding those who needed to be reminded that there was at least one indestructible constant in this rapidly changing world. There was a smell of mistrust in the square. Even weather was a suspect here. They were wearing long coats and fur hats, for they had learned to trust nothing. They would not talk or look at anyone long enough, afraid that someone might peep into their souls. The state was trying to rape their souls, they had built barricades around them. Everything belonged to the State; yet they had to have a strange communication between each other to preserve the last bastion of human freedom, the soul itself. Communism could spy on everything except this component of their life.

The SALT II agreement had been signed last week. People here could not understand how their government, which could not coexist with their own people, could be expected to live in peace with a foreign country. Jacobs sat down on the bench and looked around. There was eternal fear, despair, and distant hope all around. Now Jacobs knew what Mullinkolv meant when he was talking about suffocation. There was huge volcano underneath, covered by a very thin crust of earth holding it back. Up to now, Mullinkolv had been applying layers and layers of mud to contain the volcano from bursting into a monstrous fire. Jacobs knew it was only a matter of time before a large crack would appear, and nothing would hold back the eruption then. Molten lava would flow down, destroying everything in its path.

Communism had controlled their bodies, their minds, their property, but their souls they could not locate. What they could not locate, they denied the existence of for a number of years. But now there was a change on the way, reflected in the people displaying a combination of fear and defiance. The first one instituted by communism, the second one a necessary balancing act of the people. Now the State had threatened to confiscate this most cherished possession of the people. As if within themselves, these people had built launching pads from where they could launch their souls in well-defined, yet secret trajectories that the Communists could not locate or shoot down. Karl Marx in 1840 had visualized a classless, propertyless, and unalienated society. At that time he was so much occupied with the basic human needs that he had ignored the most basic of these, the soul itself. He had dreamed of a happy proletarian segment of society, but the reality was that he had made them the most miserable on this earth, reducing their belongings and self-respect to a speck of dirt. He had created a new class of ruling bureaucrats whose deceit, incredibility, and immorality were reflected in the faces of the so-called proletarians in the streets of Moscow.

Jacobs realized he was in a new Moscow, which was completely different from Moscow perceived from the Kremlin. People here were radiating a peculiar mixture of fear, defiance, and agony. But Jacobs was completely insulated to this radiation. As if it were needed, Mullinkolv had already provided him with an effective shield. He knew the fate of Communism and the fate of the Free World rested in his hands, for never before in the history of the world had a person, almost unaided directly, ever found himself about to make such a lasting impact on this earth.

As he finished walking down the streets of Moscow, the sun was very close to the horizon, and chill had returned to Moscow. To Moscovites, it was just like another day. Everything good around them was like dream. It gave them a good feeling, but they just could not depend upon it. When he came to Moscow, he had one reason for his mission. Here he had discovered another reason, which was most pressing. Here he had discovered the volcano about to erupt. He was running out of time. Events in America could wait but not in Moscow. It was interesting, he thought, America, which had so very little soul of its own, with morality, success, fame, and everything else for auction, to be bought and sold with the almighty dollar, had provided such a brilliant nucleus and had created a disease of souls for the Soviets. Jacobs detested all this. He knew though all the defectors from Russia with their twisted minds had built a molecule around this nucleus. It was like a chain reaction.

Last week the defense minister had defected to the U.S.A. It was positively a matter of survival for communism now. Previously brutal force could break and compromise the Moscovites. But now the game had changed. Zerenkov only understood the dictum of brutal force. Zerenkov was like a huge banyan tree, every branch a potential root. He had his roots all over the world, including the White House. He was power hungry. It was only a matter of time before he made a ruthless grab for absolute power. Jacobs didn't resent that, but what he resented was that if his mission succeeded, Zerenkov would take full credit in the Communist hierarchy, which he thought wouldn't be fair. Guaranteed, it was Zerenkov's brainchild, but from the very word go, he had nurtured it, steered it in stormy waters, and now single-handedly was ready to deliver the final blow. He would understand and tolerate the grab for power, but would not tolerate the distortion of history. He knew, unfortunately, the Communist world had always twisted, shackled, and distorted history. In this respect he could not trust either of them. And that left him no choice but to record the history in the proper perspective and leave it in a safe deposit box in Zurich, Switzerland.

Rodrigues walked into the room.
He said, "We are ready to leave the airport."
Jacobs got up and walked into the washroom. For moment he looked into the mirror. He smiled and then took off his artificial beard and mustache.

CHAPTER 15

At fifteen minutes after the morning hour of nine, the burning sun outside, which had promised a hot and dry day, was suddenly overwhelmed with dark and thick clouds that had appeared from nowhere. There was a golden hue at the top rim of the cloud. Except for that, the existence of the sun was wiped out of the sky. This was a blessing in this part of the world, for the last rainfall had been months ago. This was welcome but not enough, for it would be soaked up by the parched earth in no time, like an alcoholic who has found his first drink after being temporarily pressurized into a dry state by the unrelentless pressures of a society. Still, it was a beginning. Rodrigues had said good-bye to Jacobs at the end of the corridor where the two security men had taken over. Rodrigues was satisfied that his brief encounter with Jacobs had been rewarding. He had assured him that the security men would provide absolute protection. He would get in touch with him as soon as possible. In the meantime, Jacobs would enjoy the obscurity and security a man befitting his achievements deserved.

As the security men opened the door at the end of the corridor, through a torrential rain, he saw a white Mercedes parked close to the door. Jacobs slumped into the back seat of the car. One security man sat on the back seat on his left, the other sat in the front passenger seat. The day had been exhausting for Jacobs. From the time he had left his office and up to the time he had decoded the names and handed them over to Rodrigues, it had been a day of perpetual decision making. Some of the decisions he didn't like. Some of them were forced upon him. But he was satisfied that all the decisions had been made in a cool and reasonable manner. Given his choice, he would have liked more time for some of them, but that was a matter of personal opinion. His short acquaintance with Rodrigues was reassuring, for he had displayed an absolute authority and sense of direction. He was sure the rest of his mission would be safe in Rodrigues's hands. He was completely exhausted now. All he wanted was a deep, long sleep, for the jet lag had finally caught up with him.

The car was going over a narrow twisted road. The downpour had increased. Jacobs tried to look outside. The visibility was down to zero. The driver had bent forward and was paying undivided attention to the road between the fast-moving blades of the windshield wipers. Jacobs put a cigarette between his lips. The security man in front was quick to oblige him with the light. He put his head back and took a deep puff at his cigarette. He was a man who had a firm grip on the handle of his life. What emperors and dictators had not been able to do with their military might, he had done through his brain power. He had used intrigues to trick people, and he had twisted them into shapes of his choosing. When they stood in the way, he had eliminated them. If he had his own choice, he would have let Chimanski go but his hands were forced. Chimanski had come too close. In its own way, eliminating Chimanski had fortified his conviction that no life is precious enough when it tends to jeopardize a cause. Anyway it was all over now. He could not understand why all these thoughts were crossing his mind. It was ridiculous for a man of his logic and convictions to be intimidated by his own emotions.

The rain had somewhat abated now. Suddenly his attention was caught by a road sign. He knew it could not be true. Probably the rain had partly obscured the sign, distorted the image, and created a terrifying illusion. He looked at the security guard sitting on his left side. A sinking ache appeared in his chest. His hands were perspiring. His legs felt as if they had been stuffed with gelatin. He kept looking ahead. In the far distance, he saw a large sign. His heart was galloping at a fast pace. He felt it was going to jump out of his chest. The cigarette was between his lips, but he was neither inhaling or exhaling. The sign got closer. He tried to hold the cigarette between his fingers, which were trembling. His eyes were wide open. His mouth partly opened, for his jaw was paralysed. As the sign got closer, he turned his head imperceptibly to the right side to get a closer look. He wished it was a nightmare, but he knew it was all happening. As the sign disappeared, he turned his head to the left. Sweat was dripping from his forhead. The guard was still looking ahead.

"Where are we now?" he asked.

"State of Texas, County of Travis. Still thirty miles to go. Would you like to know specifically where we are going?" replied the security man sitting on the front passenger seat.

Jacobs was completely numb.

The man continued, "To the FBI office, Austin, where you will be specifically charged with the first-degree murders of Dr. Chimanski, Judy Starsky, and more specifically, as a principal participant in a conspiracy to commit vast human decimation."

Everything around Jacobs had collapsed. There was nothing left to salvage. The FBI had tricked him. He tried to figure out when things started to go wrong. But what was the use? Although calm outside, within he was confused and in panic.

The man in the front seat turned back, "Mr. Jacobs, I think you will remember me. We met in Switzerland when you were so generous with those golden colas. Also, I was your chauffeur when you were kidnapped. My name is Jim Reeves." He smiled and continued, "Your driver and the man on your left are both on the CIA's payroll."

Jacobs was looking ahead. The rain had slowed down to a drizzle. The sign said twenty miles to Austin. Traffic was light as usual on this out-of-the-way road. Anyone having respect for time would certainly have taken the highway. The road was mostly used by the local farmers for hauling their farm produce.

"Can I have a cigarette?" Jacobs knew, now, every move he made had to be cleared by his captors.

Reeves turned back, "Sure," and handed him a cigarette.

"Could I have my own brand?" pleaded Jacobs.

"Certainly not. Dave, take his cigarettes away. Who knows what the KGB is up to?"

The car negotiated a sharp curve. A couple of hundred feet ahead was a police car parked with its lights flashing. Two police officers were standing outside. They flagged down the car.

"John," said Reeves to the driver. "Let me handle this. Park behind the police car."

As the car came to a stop, one police officer came on each side with their guns drawn. Jim Reeves wasn't unduly disturbed.

He said, "Officer, this must be a mistake. I am an FBI agent."

The man standing on the left side shouted, "Shut up. Keep your hands on the dashboard where I can see them."

Jacobs looked to the left. The police officer had taken off his hat and was looking straight ahead at Jacobs. He couldn't believe it. He was flabbergasted. Suchlov was there to rescue him from his captors.

"Everyone out of the car," ordered Suchlov. "All three of you get into the back of the police car and Jacobs in the front."

The police car turned to the right on to a dirt road. Jacobs could not believe what was happening. He had always doubted Suchlov carrying out the most intricate mission of all. He always knew Suchlov was never short of muscle power, but to plan and carry out a mission of this caliber he had always thought was beyond his capacity. But how wrong he was. Here was Suchlov displaying his brain power.

"These bastards know everything. They know who I am," said Jacobs.

Suchlov was kneeling in the front seat, his back supported against the dashboard, with an automatic machine gun pointed at the back seat.

"Don't worry, we'll take care of them," he said.

They had hardly gone a quarter mile when they reached a thick grove of trees behind which was parked a helicopter. A large woman jumped out of the chopper.

"You three," she pointed to the agents, "lie on your face and keep your hands behind your heads." She kept her gun pointed at them.

Jim Reeves as well as the other agents knew this was their end. He should have been more careful in planning the transport of such a criminal. Anyway, it was too late now. Everything was against them. This was a desolate place. Barring a miracle, there was no reason why they should be left alive.

The woman hurried to the helicopter. "Let's get out of here," she said to Jacobs.

"Are you crazy? They know too much." Jacobs was furious. "They know who I am. They know what my mission was."

"So what?" she said.

"They have the key to the code and the names of everyone connected to my mission."

"What do you mean?" she said. The woman, who had been calm up to now, was looking at Jacobs with her large black eyes, displaying a combination of anger and panic.

"How did they get all this information?" she asked.

Jacobs was defensive. "They made me believe we landed in Nicaragua. There was this man Rodrigues who pretended to be a security minister. They even made a pretend telephone call from Zerenkov. They knew Zerenkov's code name, my code name, and they had coded names of everyone connected with my mission. With all this, they finally convinced me to give them the key to the code."

"How can you be so stupid? You have not only messed up the mission, you have opened a whole phalanx of our agents to the CIA." She was furious. "How stupid can you be? . . . You are right. That certainly asks for a change of plans. Tell me, how do we contact our agents?"

"I don't know," said Jacobs. "The CIA will monitor every contact we make with them."

"I just wanted to be sure you don't have any alternative to my plan." She was sarcastic. She put her finger on the trigger of the automatic weapon and smiled.

Jacobs felt relieved. He had convinced her to change her mind. Jacobs tried to snatch the gun from her. "Let me take care of them. These bastards have tortured me enough." His eyes displayed the ferocity and unashamed lust of a hound ready to drag a fox out of its hole. He smelled the personal satisfaction he would get out of eliminating these agents who had tricked him. He wished that Rodrigues was there too. After all, he was the man who had mainly tricked him.

The woman held onto her gun. "No, Jacobs, you don't understand. I have different plans." She ordered one of the men to start the helicopter. She took a few steps back and fired several shots. Jim Reeves lay there helpless. Seconds later he heard a moaning sound of agony. He was sure one of the CIA agents had been shot. What could he do? All he could do was to wait for his turn to be shot. There was another burst of bullets hitting the ground near him. As he lay there, the sound of the helicopter became more and more distant. Reeves waited for more shots. There was complete silence. Jim Reeves turned his head to the left. The CIA agents were still alive. John was bleeding from his leg. As he stood up to help him, he could not believe what he saw. Jacobs was lying on his face, profusely bleeding from his back. He turned his face to one side. It was a gray color, like the turned-up earth of the farm field he was lying on. Reeves could barely feel his carotids. He laid him on his back. His eyes were half open. A bead of sweat had appeared on his upper lip, which was rather symmetrically arranged. Jacobs was in a strange transition between life and death. The claws of death had dug deep into his flesh, but the angels of life had not quite let go of him. Jacobs lay there waiting in that transition zone. A stream of blood was flowing close to his head as if it had life of its own. Reeves was kneeling by his side.

Jacobs looked at Reeves, perceived him as a blurry figure, and asked, "Why did she shoot me?"

"You figure it out. She is your comrade," Reeves replied.

One of the agents who was helping his friend shot in the leg said, "Yes, why the hell did she shoot him and not us?"

Reeves smiled, "I hope you're not complaining. Help me strip him of his identity. From now onwards, he is not Stanley Jacobs, he is John Doe."

CHAPTER 16

"Mr. President, I will not. I have the responsibility to preserve the Constitution of this country." Mr. Fisher, the Chief Justice of the Supreme Court, was absolutely adamant.

President Thompson had been trying to convince him for the past hour to change his mind. "Our Constitution is becoming nothing else but suicide by popular choice. It must be occasionally bent a little to preserve it."

Replied the Chief Justice, "Mr. President, once the erosion starts, it is difficult to prevent a landslide."

President Thompson argued, "It is horrifying, yet amazing how our adversaries have manipulated and turned our own institutions against us. Don't you see while I am talking about our very survival, you are splitting hairs on the untouchability of our Constitution?"

Justice Fisher was unmoved by the argument. "Mr. President, you know very well this plea of survival has been used by those in power since times immemorial to destroy the finest institutions, and I am not about to give up on our Constitution." He shook his head from side to side. "I will not sign a blank check."

Justice Fisher paused for a while for the president's response. President Thompson said nothing.

Continued Justice Fisher, "Mr. President, let's face it. The chiefs of the FBI and CIA are either holding back information or they do not have enough evidence to ask for such powers. If I let this happen without evidence, soon we will be a police state and rapidly slide into anarchy."

The two were arguing their case as if it were a court of law, knowing well that their jury was going to be the present and succeeding generations of future Americans and whosoever wins not only in substance but in style as well, will go down in history for generations to come.

The two law-enforcement chiefs of the CIA and the FBI were sitting in the Oval Office of the White House. They merely looked at the president, who was standing under the portrait of Washington. President Thompson walked over to the FBI chief, Gerald Gibson. "All right, let's call him in."

Instead of waiting for a reply, President Thompson looked at Justice Fisher, "John, we will bring in the man who has been primarily involved with the investigation. We will order him to disclose everything. You can question him as you see fit. Then you can make up your mind."

Reeves walked into the Oval Office. He felt nervous. The world around him had revolved so fast that he was still feeling dizzy. Six hours ago he was lying face down, begging God for a miracle to happen. The miracle he was hoping for was that when the death came, it be instantaneous and painless. But now, six hours later, he was surrounded by the most powerful people on this earth, giving him their undivided attention. Events of the last few weeks had left him confused. Not only the actual happenings, but the briefings, the debriefings, the legal connotations, and the conflicting views of his superiors all contributed to his confusion. As the president introduced him to Chief Justice Fisher, he glanced outside the window for a second. He had never been inside the Oval Room before. The imperial look inside the room, he thought, was so much insulated from the world outside on the Pennsylvania Avenue.

"Jim Reeves," said the president, "I order you to disclose everything you know to Chief Justice Fisher. Do not hold anything back."

President Thompson was very presidential. History was being made. It was important for him that the game be played right, for he was up for election in the fall.

Jim Reeves sat on the chair and turned it to the side facing the chief justice. "I don't know where to start, Mr. Chief Justice.

If I tend to be confusing, please stop me."

Justice Fisher nodded.

"I am sure you have heard of Mr. Jacobs. Mr. Stanley Jacobs, the vice-president of the Sea Cola Corporation." Jim Reeves continued without waiting for an answer from Mr. Fisher. "Jacobs came to New York from Los Angeles seven years ago. His success story has been spectacular. When he came to New York, he was penniless. He started selling hot dogs on Forty-second Street. Later on he opened a couple of fast-food restaurants. Two years later he was climbing up the Sea Cola Corporation ladder. Two years ago, with his shrewd business acumen, he had become the vice-president of the company."

Interrupted Justice Fisher, "You mean in five years, he was the second most powerful man in the corporation?"

"Yes, sir. The clincher was his multibillion dollar deal in Russia. In private life he was very aloof. In business, shrewd and friendly. The president of Sea Cola described him as unpredictable but dependable. According to him, he always will deliver. So dependable as a matter of fact, for the past year he had complete control over the corporation, except for the secret formula, which the president was still guarding jealously. On Christmas Eve last year, he was shot outside a telephone booth on Forty-second Street in New York. I am convinced now, if he had not been shot then, we would certainly be in chaos today. The next morning he was to start a process that would have caused incalculable human decimation."

Justice Fisher, who up to now had been listening with a certain degree of aloofness, had changed his position. He was more attentive now. "What decimation?"

"I will come to it soon, Mr. Chief Justice." He felt confident now. "He was shot by two ordinary muggers, the type who hang around every street corner in New York. Contrary to the common belief, most of the muggers in New York have a territorial integrity."

Justice Fisher smiled.

"Now, sir, let me come to Dr. Chimanski's murder. He was a Russian Jew who came to the United States eight years ago.

He was the surgeon who operated on Jacobs when he was brought to the Metropolitan Hospital after being shot. As far as we can determine, there had never been contact between the two prior to this. The media, obviously, had taken an extraordinary interest in the shooting. Dr. Chimanski was releasing medical bulletins and giving press conferences. Among the various photographs published in the papers, Chimanski thought that a man in one of the photographs was a recognizable figure. He looked like the prison warden in Siberia, when Chimanski was a political prisoner there. Later on when Jacobs and Chimanski became friends, Chimanski tried to get Jacobs's help to establish the identity of this man.

"Jacobs tried to whitewash the whole thing, but Chimanski, fairly convinced about the identity of this man, sent a copy of the photograph to his friend, Dmitri Gustov, in Stoke-on-Trent, England, to see whether he could corroborate the identification. Two weeks later, Chimanski called his friend in England and discovered that his friend had died fifteen days earlier. That same day Chimanski called a detective agency and made an appointment with them for the next day. It seems he wanted to know whether the detective agency could discreetly establish the identity of this man. Now, Jacobs knew that Chimanski had to be stopped. He knew once he spilled the beans to the detective agency, there was no way he could control the situation."

Justice Fisher said, "How did Jacobs know that Chimanski had contacted the private situation."

"Sir, his telephone was bugged. Not the run-of-the-mill type of bug. This was a highly sophisticated, miniature, powerful transmitter we found stuck to the back of the plate in the mouthpiece of the telephone. It could transmit up to a radius of one half mile. So the same evening, Jacobs came to Chimanski's apartment. Chimanski was in the hospital performing emergency surgery. Chimanski came home at 10:00 P.M., following surgery with his girlfriend, Judy Starsky. Jacobs stayed all night, probably on the porch, waiting to get a chance. That came when Judy Starsky went to the bathroom in the morning. He murdered Chimanski with a silencer attached to the gun. At that time we could not understand why he murdered the girl as well later on in the evening.

"The FBI psychologist had made a profile of the murderer. According to the profile, the man does not commit spontaneous murders. They are all well planned. The man is very logical, cruel, calculated. He only commits murders when all other avenues are closed. The murder of Judy Starsky was falling out of this profile. But now we know why he killed her. She was in the bathroom at the time of Chimanski's murder. She didn't hear the murder weapon fired, because Jacobs had used a silencer. She asked for a towel from Chimanski. Jacobs knew if he didn't react, she was bound to come out of the bathroom to get the towel and if she found Chimanski murdered, he would lose the vital few minutes he needed to get out of the apartment complex. When Jacobs handed over the towel, she grabbed his arm, thinking that he was Chimanski. As Jacobs pulled his arm back, his arm got scratched with her nails. At that time Jacobs didn't realize what had happened. But later on, when he went home, he knew if she reported this to the police, a link could be established with him from his blood under her nails. Sir, you have to remember that at this time he was so close to his mission that he didn't want to take any chances, no matter how trivial."

Justice Fisher got up from his chair and flicked the ash off his cigar.

"Well, up to now, you have cast more than a reasonable doubt on Jacobs. Now I would like to hear about two things, motive and the smoking gun."

"Justice Fisher, sir, before I come to that, I would like to bring in one more murder."

Mr. Gibson, the chief of FBI, poured coffee for Justice Fisher and Jim Reeves.

Reeves continued, "Remember, sir, I mentioned the name Dmitri Gustov? He and Chimanski were political prisoners in the same prison in Siberia. Chimanski thought that Gustov might be able to identify the man in the photograph. After all, everyone hated this terrorist in the prison. I am not sure how Jacobs got wind that the photograph had been sent to Gustov. My impression is that since they were good friends, Chimanski might have mentioned this to him after he had sent the photograph. Jacobs had planned a trip to China during this time. He postponed his trip for three days. Those three days he spent in London and on the day Gustov was murdered, that evening he took a flight to China."

Justice Fisher had moved forward on his chair, "This is very flimsy evidence against Jacobs regarding Gustov's death."

Reeves said, "This is how it happened. Our psychologist said the man will not murder until all avenues have been exhausted. He was right. Jacobs was merely after that letter so that he could change the photograph inside with a fictitious photograph. He made a telephone call from the hotel to the post office in Stoke-on-Trent where Gustov lived. He told the postmaster that he was Dmitri Gustov, that he was going away for three days, and that there has been vandalism in the vicinity and he would appreciate it if the post was not delivered for those three days. The postmaster had no reason to suspect anything, and he complied with the request. Normally, on the fourth day, the postman would have left the post in the mailbox, but he thought he would inquire about the vandalism. During each of these days, Jacobs would drive from London to Stoke-on-Trent in his hired car because he did not want to take any chances. The fourth day, he thought all he had to do was to pick up the letter, change the photograph, and put it back again. But then he had to change his plans. The postman delivered the mail by hand. So Jacobs rang the bell. As Gustov opened the door, he walked in. Gustov had been dictating his memoirs in Siberia for a local newspaper in his dining room. Before he opened the door, he forgot to switch off the tape recorder. This is how the conversation went."

Reeves pulled a small tape cassette out of his pocket and placed it in the small tape recorder lying on the table. "Justice Fisher, there is a lot of extraneous noise on this tape, because the conversation was being recorded from the next room. We had to amplify the sound in the FBI lab. This is how the conversation went:"

"Please don't shoot me. I will give you anything you want."

Reeves stopped the tape recorder and pointed out to Justice Fisher that that was Gustov. He started the tape all over again.

"Please don't shoot me. I will give you anything you want."

"Keep your hands up. Turn around slowly. Sit down. Do you know where these letters are from?"

"One is a football pool. One I know is from the USA."

"Who in the USA?"

"What is this all about, please? Are you from Scotland Yard?"

"Never mind. Don't force me to use this gun. Who from the USA?"

There was a sound of letter opening.

"Can you recognize the man in the photograph?"

"Sir, what is this all about? Would you please explain it to me?"

"Answer my question. Do you know this man in the photograph?"

"Can't say I know him."

"Do you remember seeing him in Siberia when you were a prisoner?"

"Of course, I know who you are. Put that gun down. I am on your side. You are from the Jewish organization that hunts down criminals who committed genocide against the Jews . . . This man is a prison warden. How could I forget this brute? Absolute terror. Put that gun down, will you? What would you like, tea or coffee?"

Suddenly there was the noise of two shots in succession.

"These spineless creatures are messing up this planet."

Reeves shut the tape recorder off. "We have run voice tests on the tape. Experts say they coincide with Jacobs's and Gustov's."

"The photograph they are talking about is a copy of a clipping from one of the newspapers that Chimanski had sent to him."

Justice Fisher lit a fresh cigar. "Who and why was this man hanging around the hospital?"

"Because he was Jacobs's contact man from the Russian

Embassy. His name is Andrea Suchlov. Officially he is naval attaché to the Russian Embassy. Why he was coming to the hospital when Jacobs got shot, we don't know for sure. My guess is, number one, he wanted to know how serious the injury was, and number two, Jacobs probably had some significant documents with him when he was shot."

Justice Fisher had crossed his legs and was showing intense curiosity, which was against his cultivated habit of maintaining an expressionless stance.

"Sir, as I said before, these muggers in New York have their own code of behavior. They only operate in specified areas. Through our underground connections, we were able to contact the muggers. Jacobs had given the police a wrong description. We had a glimpse into Jacobs's wallet. It cost us one hundred dollars to look into his wallet. Who says crime doesn't pay?"

Justice Fisher smiled.

"When we ripped the wallet apart, inside were numerals and letters mixed together, obviously some coded message. But our greatest break came when a man was doing what he should not have been doing. Sea Cola Corporation had obtained the services of a protection agency to safeguard against the kidnapping of the key Sea Cola officials. Stewart, a smart but unconventional man, was assigned to protect Jacobs. I knew Stewart before. He was employed by the FBI. Three years ago he was fired from the FBI because he would not follow any rules. Last week of February, Jacobs had gone to Zurich to attend a conference. Stewart followed him around without his knowledge. It seems partly because Stewart was getting bored and partly because his security was becoming a big risk, that Stewart decided to step over his traditional security measures. He bugged Jacobs's telephone in the hotel room. He put powerful miniature transmitters under his coat lapels. These transmitters are about the size of a grain of rice, highly specialized classified equipment of the CIA. How Stewart got hold of this equipment, I have no idea. In Zurich, Jacobs came out of the opera house and went across the lobby into a telephone booth. Stewart had recorded the conversation on tape. Please remember he was only able to record what Jacobs was saying."

Reeves put the tape recorder on again.

"There has been a change of plans."

Pause . . .

"He is taking an early vacation, three weeks from now."

Pause . . .

"Soon after I know my mission is successful, I would like to get out."

Pause . . .

"Blue Vampire says that you have the key to the code. I will leave the new code on page 150 of the telephone book. You leave the key to the code on the same page."

"As Stewart watched, Jacobs went through the crowded lobby to the telephone booth on the other side of the lobby, and a chubby man wearing dark glasses went over to the telephone booth from where Jacobs had made the call. They both opened the telephone books and within seconds were gone. This man, we have since recognized. Again, he is Andrea Suchlov, naval attaché at the Russian Embassy in New York.

"Justice Fisher, I have been narrating the sequences as they occurred, but as a matter of fact, I got involved with the investigation at this stage. Stewart called me and raised suspicions regarding Jacobs. Stewart's biggest problem was credibility. I found it difficult to believe the story, but I thought it would be worth checking into. So I went into Jacobs's background. I found he and Chimanski were close friends. By now, Chimanski was dead. I went over Chimanski's apartment with a fine-tooth comb. There was one unopened telephone bill lying in his mailbox. Except for two telephone calls, the rest were made to the hospital. One was to Stoke-on-Trent, to his friend, Gustov. The other was to a detective agancy in Manhattan. Both calls were made the evening before he was killed. The detective agency had no idea what he wanted to discuss with them.

"So by now, Chimanski, Judy Starsky, and Gustov were all dead. I talked to the local police. They are still convinced that Doctor Chimanski and Judy were murdered by her husband. He is still in jail awaiting trial. We looked into the background of all three victims and found nothing in common. They were not politically motivated. They were not in contact with Russians,

Chinese, CIA, or any other espionage organization. By now, the CIA and FBI agreed that Jacobs was on industrial espionage activity and was obviously working to steal the jealously guarded Sea Cola formula. We put this theory to Williams, the president and owner of the Sea Cola Corporation. He refused to believe us, but was ready to cooperate with us.

"In the meantime, Stewart had been following Jacobs in Zurich. He had discovered that he had been repeatedly going to the National Bank in Zurich and depositing something in his safety deposit box. Undoubtedly, our next step was to look into that box. We provided Stewart with technology to do exactly that."

Justice Fisher asked, "Did you actually break into the bank in Zurich? A neutral country?"

"No sir, the CIA and FBI didn't. Stewart did it as a private citizen."

Justice Fisher thought that was amusing.

"To cut it short, we used a laser-beam technology. We juggled around for a couple of days with the boxes. When we looked into the box, we found forty-seven small Golden Sea Cola bottles, each six ounces in size, the type with which Sea Cola proposed to celebrate their hundredth anniversary. At the bottom of the box, there were forty-eight microfilms with coded messages. At that time, we had no idea what that meant since we had no key to the code. We sent those bottles to the CIA lab. The following morning Stewart became critically ill and died within twenty-four hours.

"Now we knew there was more than industrial espionage. We followed Jacobs closely, and that led us to his country estate in the Mohawk Valley in New York State."

Mr. Gibson unfolded a white screen. He put the slide projector on. He projected a slide showing a huge colonial house.

Said Reeves, "Sir, this is his country estate, a huge mansion surrounded by thirty acres of farm land. He spent most of the weekends in this retreat. Business analysts had thought that his Sea Cola strategies originated here. But now we have proof that this was the nerve center of his espionage activities."

Gibson projected the next slide.

Reeves continued, "This is a dish antenna on his estate. It is so powerful that it is capable of capturing any relays from the satellites over the Western Hemisphere. Every Saturday, 9:00 P.M. to 11:00 P.M., Eastern Time, Radio Moscow, through satellite, would beam Russian music. First alphabet and last alphabet of each song was their coded message to him. Last message we decoded was, 'Blue Vampire will rescue soon. Contact Rodrigues.'

"We sent our spies into Russia. What we found was unbelievable. Jacobs wasn't American. He was a Russian born in Moscow. He was thirty-five years old and had been vigorously trained by the KGB for five years prior to being implanted in Los Angeles, where he took the identity of a man who seemed to have completely disappeared. This man's name now we know was David Smith. He immediately came to New York as David Smith and within a couple of months changed his name to Stanley Jacobs, which was a simple procedure. From a legal point of view, all he had to do was to put an announcement in the paper that he was going to change his name. It is as simple as that. He lay low for a couple of years and the rest of his success story you already know.

"Once we established that he was a Russian spy, we knew he was up to something more than an industrial espionage. In the meantime, there was a conference going to be held in Zurich in the middle of March. The topic of the conference was the effect of food additives. Jacobs was there too, in the Sea Cola stalls. As the scientists were going around, Jacobs passed on those forty-eight bottles to different scientists from all over the Western world. We had inserted radioactive tracers in each bottle so that we could keep a close tab on these bottles. They are famous and some are top scientists in the United States, Britain, West Germany, France, Italy, and the Netherlands. In the meantime we had tests back from the CIA lab that showed the bottles contained a deadly virus, a slow kind of virus, which normally takes about two weeks to activate, but if taken along with alcohol, it can kill within a few hours. The virus causes severe spreading infection all over the body, including the brain. Our scientists tested it against all the known antibiotics. There is none effective against it. The only thing effective is the inoculation against the virus. Experiments with animals showed a 99 percent death rate and 1 percent surviving were severely crippled. Now we know how Stewart died. His overwhelming curiosity killed him. He took a bottle of Sea Cola out of the safety box while he was bringing the box from the bank. Same night he brought a girl to his room, who unknowingly mixed rum and Sea Cola for him. Our agents in Russia have been able to track down the scientist who discovered this deadly virus. He is in a mental asylum. He had discovered this while doing genetic manipulations of the viruses.

"The day before yesterday, April the second, at 4:00 P.M., when Jacobs was being driven to the airport, he was kidnapped. This kidnapping was arranged by the Russians."

"Wait a minute." There was no change in the expression on Justice Fisher's face. "You mean Russian agents are hanging around freely in the streets of New York?"

"No, sir," said Reeves, "they use the capitalist system to their advantage. There are some underground organizations in this country who will do anything you want them to do, provided you are willing to pay the right price. And more important, with no questions asked. We contacted the people who kidnapped him. It cost us ten thousand dollars. It seems they had no idea who they were kidnapping for and they could not care less, so long as they were paid one hundred thousand dollars for forty-five minutes' work."

Justice Fisher smiled a little. "I never knew criminals had strict rules and ethical standards. Anyway, go on."

"Within two hours of his kidnapping, ransom demands started coming in for two million dollars. For twenty-four hours, the FBI was negotiating for his release. The next day, I mean yesterday, at 8:00 P.M. they put him on a Nicaraguan air flight from Newark to Managua. They had changed his identity and appearance."

Justice Fisher intervened, "Mr. Reeves, slow down a little. This could not be true. Didn't you hear the 6:00 P.M. news yesterday? Jacobs's charred body, burnt beyond recognition, was found in a parked car near the United Nations Building, with a note saying that the FBI had broken the negotiations for his release. The medical examiner has established his identity from his dental records."

Reeves replied, "That is true, sir. This was a brilliant diversion set up by KGB, and it worked for a while. As a matter of fact, the FBI called off the investigation at 5:00 P.M. yesterday. The watch we discovered on the dead body belonged to Jacobs, so did the partially burnt-out shoes. But to me it didn't make sense. If they wanted to kill him, why would they burn the body? More likely they would shoot him and leave him in an alley. I called the medical examiner. The dental records he is talking about are from Los Angeles. I called the hospital where Jacobs was operated on by Dr. Chimanski four months ago. They said Chimanski had used stainless-steel wire to close deeper tissues in his abdomen. The medical examiner says there is no trace of this wire in the burnt-out dead body. So we knew the dead body was of our original David Smith. So the FBI investigation was on again. The KGB had diverted our attention so that they could get him out of the country. From here on our task was easy. We looked for him on all the aircraft leaving the country and found him on a flight to Managua."

Justice Fisher relit his half-finished cigar. "That certainly was a brilliant ploy by the KGB."

"So when the aircraft landed at Houston and all the passengers went to the transition lounge, we switched his bag and the bag of the man accompanying him to different but similar-looking aircraft. We filled the aircraft with FBI and CIA agents and landed him at a small airport near Austin, Texas. We made him believe he had landed in Managua. There, with considerable difficulty, he gave us the key to the code and confessed to various murders. What finally convinced him was a pretend telephone call from the Chief of the KGB, Zerenkov, and the fact that we had the coded names of the agents connected with his mission. Zerenkov, Suchlov, and he were the only three who knew the coded names of the agents, plus there was a copy lying in the Swiss bank deposit box.

"After we had extracted all the information from him, we

were taking him to the FBI office. We don't know who passed the information to the Russians. They knew he was being transported. They commandeered a police car and came to rescue him with a helicopter. Everything went all right. At that time Jacobs told his rescuers that we had extracted all the information from him, including the key to the coded names of the agents connected with his mission. They knew then, the CIA and FBI would be monitoring these agents very thoroughly. So there was no way left for the KGB to contact these agents and tell them to be on their guard. Their next move was to shoot Jacobs and to bring this story to the newspapers and the television media, so that agents would know that something had drastically gone wrong with the mission.

"Consequently, Jacobs was shot and died immediately. I stripped him of his identity. Up to now we have been able to convince the local authorities not to release any information about him. His body is lying in Austin as John Doe. There have been several calls to newspapers and television stations, which we have been able to screen out. The Russians are desperate to get the news that Jacobs was a Russian spy who has been killed into the press, and we are determined to keep it out. The next few days are important to us. We want to monitor the agents whose names Jacobs has provided us with."

Justice Fisher was supporting his head on both hands, shaking it from side to side. "Unbelievable. It's unbelievable. How close we were to devastation by biological means."

"Yes, sir. We were very close. The irony of the story is that if those two black thugs hadn't shot Jacobs, and if Stewart hadn't used unconventional methods, more than one-third of the Western world would have been wiped out. By the way, Chief Justice Fisher, one of the names we got from Jacobs is a Justice of the Supreme Court."

Justice Fisher showed no emotion. "So was Jacobs able to introduce the virus into the Sea Cola?"

"He thought he did. But we had him under close surveillance for the past two months. Mr. Williams, the president of the Sea Cola Corporation, had the whole plant restructured so that whatever was introduced by Jacobs never got into the bottles. Instead, it was going into the CIA scientific labs."

Justice Fisher had dug his elbows into the armrests of the chair. He was rocking the chair. He had closed his eyes, not so much to concentrate, but to shut himself from reality. Then he opened his eyes suddenly, "That means millions of people would have died."

"Rough estimate is that fifty million people would have died."

Justice Fisher had partly recovered from the shock. "Why was he passing those bottles to the scientists in that conference in Switzerland?"

"The plan was to make anti-viral serum. Under the cap of each bottle was the microfilm, with coded names of all the persons to whom this serum was to be administered. Our scientists tell us that once the serum was made, it could be given by mixing it with any drink. The motive was to produce chaos in Western society. While the people in the Western world were dying, the Communist stooges would grab power. Imagine, sir, fifty million people dead, probably another fifty million sick."

"Have you any idea who are the co-conspirators of this?"

"We know the Chief of the KGB, Zerenkov, is a co-conspirator. Whether anyone else is involved in this, we don't know. Our investigation is still continuing."

Justice Fisher got up from his chair. He shook Reeves's hand. "Mr. Reeves I want to thank you for your brilliance in uncovering this conspiracy to obliterate millions of humans. I completely agree with the president now. What powers do you want me to give to the FBI?"

"I have a list of the names. One, as I said, is a Justice of the Supreme Court, plus a lot of attorneys, some doctors, some businessmen, and union officials. We don't know what their exact link is with Moscow, but this is the list that Jacobs gave us when he thought he was in Nicaragua. I beg you to grant us permission to bug their homes, bug their cars, bug their telephones, and bug their wives and children. I ask for this simply because the stakes are too high. I also request authority to intercept and manipulate all communications going to major media networks and every newspaper in this country. As you know, once news gets into the newspaper office, there is no way any of us can stop it from getting printed. After Jacobs died I stripped him of his identity. He is lying in a morgue in Austin. We request that his body be transferred to the FBI. We want these powers for one week so that we can watch those agents closely because, as far as they are concerned, Jacobs has escaped to Russia and the mission is still rolling."

Justice Fisher nodded. "You can go ahead."

President Thompson had walked over to the window overlooking the Pennsylvania Avenue. He knew a cold wind was going to blow from Moscow this winter, but he was prepared for it. He picked up his binoculars and focused on the far end of the lawn. Two fat squirrels were nibbling on peanuts thrown by the tourists. There were a young boy and a girl throwing the peanuts. The boy had his hand around her shoulders. She was clinging to his waist. He looked at her with those penetrating, lingering eyes. She responded by looking back at him. He said something to her. Perhaps the boy had promised the whole world to his girl. It was the same world that, tomorrow evening, President Thompson was going to promise to the country in his election speech. But there was one big difference. The boy sincerely believed in his promise, whereas President Thompson was going to make a promise he did not believe in.